Shadows Across the Sun

Have you read

Under the Cherry Blossom?

Find out how Hana and Kimi's adventure begins in the first instalment of Maya Healy's captivating quartet.

Available now

Coming Soon:

Between Heaven and Earth

Sword Against the Sky

Shadows Across the Sun

Maya Healy

OXFORD
UNIVERSITY PRESS

Special thanks to Helen Hart.

Thanks also to Dr Phillip Harries of The Queen's College,
Oxford, for his invaluable advice and expertise.

OXFORD
UNIVERSITY PRESS

L 211, 582

Great Clarendon Street, Oxford OX2 6DP

Oxford University Press is a department of the University of Oxford.
It furthers the University's objective of excellence in research, scholarship,
and education by publishing worldwide in

Oxford   New York

Auckland   Cape Town   Dar es Salaam   Hong Kong   Karachi
Kuala Lumpur   Madrid   Melbourne   Mexico City   Nairobi
New Delhi   Shanghai   Taipei   Toronto

With offices in

Argentina   Austria   Brazil   Chile   Czech Republic   France   Greece
Guatemala   Hungary   Italy   Japan   Poland   Portugal   Singapore
South Korea   Switzerland   Thailand   Turkey   Ukraine   Vietnam

Oxford is a registered trade mark of Oxford University Press
in the UK and in certain other countries

British Library Cataloguing in Publication Data
Data available

ISBN: 978-0-19-273311-5
1 3 5 7 9 10 8 6 4 2

Printed in Great Britain
Paper used in the production of this book is a natural,
recyclable product made from wood grown in sustainable forests.
The manufacturing process conforms to the environmental
regulations of the country of origin.

For Pam.
More than an aunt.
A true friend.

Prologue

News travels fast, carried across the kingdom by farmers, peasants, rich men, and thieves.

'Have you heard about the treachery and terror?' they whisper, gathering together at dusk, on street corners, or by the fireside. 'Have you heard about the bloodshed?'

I draw closer, ears straining, as I listen to tales of the evil *jito*, Lord Steward of the southern part of the Kai Province: an innocent family massacred, burning arrows flickering through the night sky, a people's suffering.

The details change with each retelling, but the story remains the same. The truth cannot be subdued.

It is a story I could never forget—burned into my memory by pain and blood. The *jito* is my uncle. It was my family that was massacred.

And I have carried that truth with me, since the moment my sister Hana and I witnessed our treacherous uncle stab our father in the back.

From that day on, my life was consumed by the mission to bring honour back to the Yamamoto name. The only hope for the future was our little brother, Moriyasu, the rightful *jito* now that Father was dead.

Hana and I clung to that truth lingering in our hearts: one day we would be reunited with what was left of our family.

But what is the truth?

Those stories around the fire? The honour of a family name? The promises of a friend?

I know now that nothing is ever what it seems.

chapter 1

It was shortly after dawn, and my sister Hana and I were in our small room in the servants' quarter of our samurai training school.

A fresh early-morning breeze blew in through an open bamboo screen, bringing with it the scent of cherry blossom petals crushed by the overnight rain. Outside, the sky was slowly lightening, and droplets of water still sparkled on the leaves and flowers in the garden.

Hana and I knelt opposite each other, our hands resting lightly on our thighs. We were dressed in our usual servants' outfits of a short blue jacket, blue breeches, and bare feet. We had been meditating quietly, but now it was time to face the day ahead. Tonight would be very hard.

'Master Goku's funeral . . . ' Hana murmured. Her voice sounded tight, as if she was close to tears. 'I don't think I can bear it, Kimi.'

I reached out and smoothed her long hair hanging loose over her shoulder like silky black rope. 'We have to bear it,' I said gently. 'Master Goku is dead, and there is nothing we can do to change that.'

'I wish Mother was here,' Hana whispered.

'I wish that, too,' I said.

An image of Mother as I had last seen her blazed across my mind. It was dusk, and she had been sitting with Father and Uncle in the rock garden. As Hana and I had led our brother Moriyasu away to his bedchamber, I'd glanced back over my shoulder and seen Mother smiling at Father. Her face had been so serene and confident, full of strength and wisdom.

My heart twisted at the thought of how happy we had been then. Before my uncle had ripped us apart.

Would I ever see Mother again? My soul lifted with the hope that one day Mother, Moriyasu, Hana, and I could be together for ever. I thought of the bamboo sword hiding in our storage basket, my little brother's favourite toy, and renewed my vow to return it to him.

I dragged my thoughts back to the present. 'One day at a time,' I said firmly, more to myself than Hana. 'We just need to get through tonight. Mother's letter will soon arrive, telling us where to meet her.'

Before he took his last breath, Master Goku had told us of his cedarwood box full of our mother's letters. A true friend, he had risked everything to arrange for our reunion. Mother had said she would send one more instruction to tell us how to find her.

One final letter. One more precious paper scroll.

'Then we can go to her,' Hana said, 'and be a family again . . .'

The sound of hurrying feet came from the hallway outside.

'Everybody up!' came the deep, rumbling voice of Mister Choji, the head servant. Since Master Goku's death, Choji had taken over the *dojo* and now everyone addressed him more respectfully as Mister Choji.

Hana and I exchanged a horrified glance. If Mister Choji came into our room now, he would see our long hair tumbling over our

3

shoulders and know in an instant that we were girls.

'We're coming!' I called out as we leapt to our feet, scrambling to twist up our hair into boyish top-knots.

'I need you all, right away.' Mister Choji seemed in a panic. 'The *jito* is coming and he wants the funeral to take place immediately!'

The *jito*? The blood in my veins pulsed furiously. Mister Choji meant Lord Hidehira, our uncle. The man who had murdered our father and brothers. And now he was disrupting the arrangements for the funeral of our murdered Master. The thought made anger fill my heart like black smoke. How dare he? When his own son had been responsible for Master Goku's death!

I paused at the door, and turned back to see Hana's shaking hands quickly secure her hair with a pointed metal hairpin. I raised my eyebrows to ask if she was ready, and when she nodded I slid back the bamboo screen and came face to face with Mister Choji.

He was a gruff, good-natured man, round-faced and stocky, with black hair which he wore pulled into the traditional samurai's oiled tail, tightly folded on the top of his head. On our arrival, Mister Choji had taken Hana and me under his wing, affectionately calling us 'skinny boys' as he fed us hearty meals of soup and noodles.

'Quickly, boys! We are not prepared for the *jito*,' Mister Choji said. 'I need one of you to ring the bell and wake the students, while the other goes to the kitchens and brings out the ceremonial tea bowls.' He clapped his hands and turned away in a flurry of pale grey kimono robes. 'Hurry!'

'I'll ring the bell,' I said to my sister.

Hana nodded. 'I will prepare the tea bowls and meet you in the kitchens afterwards.'

We dashed after Mister Choji, who was striding along the narrow hallway. He knocked on wooden door frames as he went, calling out to the sleeping occupants. Screen doors slid back, revealing yawning boys in breeches with tousled hair.

'What's happening?' someone asked. 'Are we under attack?'

'Get up! Get dressed!' Mister Choji cried, clapping his hands. 'We've just had word that the *jito* is coming—the funeral will be this morning.'

'The *jito* is coming . . . ' the urgent whisper carried along the hallway, carried from one room to the next. 'This morning?' servants asked in confusion. Master Goku's body was to be moved this evening to the temple, and the funeral wasn't supposed to take place until tonight.

Through an open doorway I caught a glimpse of my friend Ko rubbing his eyes, and then Hana and I were outside, thrusting our feet into our sandals and racing along the covered walkway which led to the gardens. Hana headed for the kitchens, the soles of her sandals flashing as she hurried. I turned and ran along gravel pathways that led through the *dojo* gardens, ducking beneath over-hanging branches.

As I reached the bell tower I saw the sun rising, a bright crimson ball painting the sky pink and orange. I ran up the bell tower steps and hauled on the rope to swing the wooden beam against the metal. The beam was heavy and it took two strong tugs to get it swinging. At last the deep sonorous sound rang out, echoing across the gardens and reverberating against the far walls of the *dojo*.

I kept pulling, ringing the bell again and again.

From my vantage point I could see the *dojo* laid out beneath me: neatly swept pathways cut through green moss gardens; pools of still water reflected the early-morning sky; curving red rooftops rose up from the foliage like the wings of exotic birds. Trees clung to the hillside behind the *dojo*, interrupted only by the long path that led up to the temple.

This place had become home, a haven from the

man that hunted us. But now with Goku gone, I didn't know if we could still be safe here.

Stilling the rope, I watched as screen doors flew back in the students' quarters. Boys of all ages hurried onto the walkways, some still tying up their hair while they ran to their duties. Others looked as if they had been up for hours, meditating or practising their *kata* movements. Junior masters in black robes quickly joined them.

Everyone was awake now, and the *dojo* took on an air of bustling purpose. As I headed back towards the kitchens, I realized that someone had fallen into step beside me.

'I've heard the news,' a voice said. I glanced up into the concerned face of my friend Tatsuya, the only person other than Master Goku that Hana and I had trusted with our secret. He was dressed formally for the funeral, his short white kimono jacket neatly pressed and the soft fabric of his black *hakama* trousers pooling around his feet. A long curved sword in its scabbard was tucked into his sash.

'Where's Hana?' he asked as he limped slightly with every other step. His ankle was still hurting him after Ken-ichi, Uncle's son, had sabotaged him at the tournament, but it was healing quickly.

'She's in the kitchens,' I replied, 'preparing for the *Kaminari*'s arrival.' *Kaminari*, meaning thunder, was the nickname the people had given to Uncle because he raged through their villages like a storm.

'I won't let anything happen to either of you,' Tatsuya said.

I paused at the end of the walkway and bowed to him. 'Thank you, Tatsuya.' It was good to know we had a friend.

'Do you think Hidehira is coming here to look for Ken-ichi?' Tatsuya asked as we walked on.

'Maybe,' I replied. Then another thought made me shudder. 'Or maybe someone has seen through our disguise and he is coming here to find us.'

Tatsuya shook his head. 'No, he can't have discovered you. Just try to stay out of his way.'

We made our way over a low wooden footbridge and came to a fork in the path. Several students were gathered there, listening to one of the junior masters give them instructions for the rescheduled funeral. Their faces were sombre.

'I should go,' I said. 'Mister Choji will need my help.'

Tatsuya nodded and I hurried away to join Hana in the kitchens. I found her laying out tea bowls on a lacquered tray. Mister Choji caught sight of me and gestured impatiently. 'Skinny boy, come with me! And bring your brother! It is almost time for me to go to the main courtyard and receive Lord Hidehira. You will attend me!'

My thoughts began to race. Attending Mister Choji meant standing close while he greeted Uncle. Close enough for Uncle to recognize us if he looked closely. We would have to be careful not to draw attention to ourselves. Hana looked anxious. We both knew that if Uncle realized who we were, all would be lost.

'Don't just stand there, skinny boys!' Mister Choji cried, turning and heading for the door in a flurry of grey robes. 'Follow me!'

We leaped to obey, following Mister Choji out of the kitchens and along the walkways. The last few students were streaming towards the archway leading to the main courtyard, their black *hakama* trousers fluttering as they ran.

As we passed one of the moss gardens, Master Choji slowed his step to allow Hana and me to catch up. 'You seem surprised that I have chosen you to attend me this morning,' he said as we walked beside him. 'Master Goku thought highly of you, so it is fitting for you both to stand behind me as I formally greet His Lordship in the courtyard. Afterwards we will proceed to the pavilion in the moss garden for the *cho na yoriai* tea ceremony. Is that understood?'

'Yes, Mister Choji,' we murmured. A memory flashed in my mind. The last time I had been in that pavilion, I had almost assassinated my uncle. Master Goku had stopped me and taught me the only honourable way to avenge my father was to challenge Uncle openly.

Running footsteps crunched the gravel on the pathway behind us and we quickly moved aside to let two of the younger students past.

'Hurry now,' Mister Choji called to them. 'Don't be late.'

'Yes, Mister Choji!' the boys said, bowing quickly before they raced on towards the main courtyard.

Mister Choji watched them go, and then turned back to Hana and me.

'Today will be a difficult day for the students,' he said. 'It's almost unbearable to think that we will be saying goodbye to Master Goku for the last time.'

I bowed my head, suddenly so full of grief that I could not trust myself to speak.

'This situation will be awkward for Lord Hidehira, too,' Mister Choji went on. I thought I caught a note of disapproval in his voice when he said Uncle's name. 'Long ago, Lord Hidehira attended this school. With Ken-ichi responsible for Goku's death, the Lord Steward will feel the pain of Goku's death twice over—the loss of his Master, and the disgrace of his son.'

'Yes, Mister Choji,' I said again. But privately I did not think Uncle was the sort of man to feel pain or loss. He had killed his own brother! He had no feelings. Nothing but his desire for power mattered to him.

We came to the wooden archway which led into the main sandy courtyard. Two guards in leather armour stood either side of the main gate, their iron helmets gleaming.

Mister Choji paused for a moment, closing his eyes and stilling himself. Then he gave Hana and me a nod as we stepped through the archway.

Before us were row upon row of seated students.

There were about a hundred students and teachers gathered altogether. Although they were trying to be quiet and respectful as they awaited the arrival of the *jito*, the wide open space seemed to pulse with their energy and anticipation. The tallest students stood at the back against the rear wall of the courtyard, their black belts showing their seniority. The younger ones knelt in the formal *seiza* position at the front, their hands resting lightly on their knees.

Mister Choji made his way to the centre of the courtyard ready to welcome our important visitor. Hana and I hurried to stand behind him, our heads bowed. A hush descended. The only sounds were the breeze whispering through the pine trees surrounding the *dojo* and the gentle splash of a waterfall in one of the gardens nearby.

A conch-shell horn sounded, signalling the approach of the *jito*. As the sound faded away, the muffled thunder of horses' hooves rose in the still morning air.

I glanced at Hana. Her face was composed but pale. I tried taking a deep breath to calm myself, but inside I was in turmoil at the thought of seeing Uncle Hidehira once more.

The thundering horses' hooves came closer. I opened my eyes as more than ten mounted samurai galloped in through the open gates, their red silk *mon* badges gleaming at their shoulders. Glittering swords were strapped to their waists and quivers of arrows bristled at their backs.

The samurai's horses churned up the carefully swept sand as they wheeled and spread out to line the walls either side of the courtyard. Through the

gates behind them came an ornate black lacquered palanquin carried on the shoulders of four
bearers in scarlet livery, its white silk curtains rippling in the breeze.

The sight of this palanquin used to thrill me
with anticipation of my father's appearance, but
now, knowing the evil man that would emerge,
all I felt was disgust.

The palanquin came to a halt in the centre of
the courtyard just as more samurai on horseback
came cantering in through the gates. Their captain
gave a curt order and the two guards hurried to
close the gates behind them.

The bearers set the palanquin down and my
body tensed. Beside me, Hana stood as still as a
marble statue, her gaze fixed to the ground in
front of her.

A large, powerful hand appeared at the curtains, crushing the fragile silk. The curtains were
roughly pulled aside and Uncle Hidehira
appeared. His thin-lipped smile didn't reach his
dark eyes. Loathing filled my soul.

Mister Choji made a gesture and, as one, the
school bowed. Hana and I placed our hands on
our thighs and bent low.

As we rose again, Uncle Hidehira stepped down
from the palanquin. He straightened up, hands on

hips, his broad shoulders dwarfing the guards who stood on either side. He surveyed the assembled school. His gaze seemed to penetrate deep into the soul of each person he looked at.

I kept my head bowed, but peeked at Uncle from beneath my eyelashes, studying him carefully. Father always said, *Know your opponent as well as you know yourself because that is how you will discover his weakness.*

Usually Uncle wore robes of glossy red silk to signify his important role as *jito* but now he was dressed traditionally in white for the funeral. The many layers of his luxurious kimono moved heavily as he walked across the courtyard towards Mister Choji. His black hair had been shaved at the front, then oiled and folded in an ornate ceremonial style. Two swords—one long, one slightly shorter—were stuck into his stiffened *obi* sash.

Uncle returned Mister Choji's respectful bow with a slight bow of his own, and I guessed that he felt it was beneath him to show a mere head servant too much honour.

The two men greeted each other formally in low voices. I could see tension on my uncle's face. His confident air was betrayed by the new lines on his forehead. Perhaps it was us, the surviving witnesses of his treachery, that weighed on his mind. I hoped it was.

A sharp thought filled my mind: I had an advantage over Uncle. Despite all his power, I knew something he didn't. My mother and brother were alive and safe—and soon we would be together again. I was sure of it.

Hana shifted beside me and I reached out to her, touching her fingers in our secret signal of kinship.

Mister Choji bowed to Uncle Hidehira once more, robes rippling. 'Will you do me the honour of accepting a bowl of tea in our pavilion, Lord Hidehira?'

Uncle Hidehira gazed at him for a moment, his eyes as black and expressionless as a lizard's. 'No tea, thank you.'

My heart began to pump harder. By refusing tea, Uncle was dishonouring Mister Choji in front of the whole school!

A few of the students exchanged shocked glances and I saw that the back of Mister Choji's neck had flushed red.

'I think a tour of the school would be more appropriate,' Uncle Hidehira said at last. 'If it is your intention to take over here as Master, then I want to see what your plans are, and how you intend to expand and improve this *dojo*.'

Mister Choji bowed low. 'Of course, Lord Steward,' he said. 'Please follow me.'

As he turned, he nodded at Hana and me to show that we should follow, and together the men walked across the sunny courtyard, gravel crunching underfoot. Hana and I fell into step behind them. At a signal from Uncle Hidehira two of his personal guard, samurai with fearsome horned helmets and hard leather armour, walked behind us.

'The servant has become Master,' Uncle Hidehira said as soon as we were away from the main courtyard.

Mister Choji inclined his head slightly. 'Your Lordship knows that I did not seek this honour,' he said gruffly. 'It was the wish of the junior masters and students. They wanted someone who knew Goku's work, and would carry on in the same tradition.'

'Goku's work was good,' Uncle Hidehira agreed with a nod. 'He was wise and skilled. I was counting on him to train the captains of my army.' He cast a sharp sideways glance at Choji. 'May I count on you in the same way, Choji?'

'Of course, Your Lordship. I will serve you just the same way as Goku did.'

I smiled to myself at this. My uncle did not know how Goku refused to serve Uncle, how he had kept us concealed. And I felt sure that Mister Choji *would* do the same.

Uncle Hidehira looked satisfied. 'Good,' he said, as they followed the curving path. 'Because I have great plans for my estates. Great plans!'

The sound of hurrying feet came along the pathway behind us, and I turned my head to see the hands of the two samurai guards going instantly to the hilts of their swords, but then they relaxed as a messenger came trotting around the curve in the path, his clothes and armour dusty from the road. I realized that the guards' reaction meant that Uncle was constantly on guard for a threat to his power.

He should be, I thought.

The messenger bowed low. 'Forgive the intrusion, Mister Choji, but I have brought a message.'

Mister Choji nodded and beckoned. 'Please come forward.'

My blood began to race when I caught a glimpse of the tightly rolled paper scroll in the messenger's hand. This could be the letter from Mother!

I glanced at Hana and saw that her gaze was fixed on the messenger.

Mister Choji held out his hand to take the scroll, but Uncle Hidehira stopped him and my breath caught in my throat.

'You should not forget your place, Choji,' he said sharply. 'A servant does not assume all the authority of Master overnight. The appointment of Master of this *dojo* comes from the *jito* himself.'

I held my breath, stunned by Uncle's tone. As Mister Choji bowed I could see the flash of anger in his eyes, and I knew he was holding himself tightly in check.

Uncle Hidehira seized the scroll from the messenger, half crushing the fragile paper. This was the worst possible situation. I now prayed that this would be the vegetable accounts or a *dojo* application—anything other than the letter that we had been waiting for, the letter that would expose everything!

As the messenger bowed and hurried away, Uncle slit the wax seal with his thumbnail and tore away the scarlet ribbon that bound it. Slowly, he unrolled the curling paper.

From where I was standing I had a clear view of the thick black brush strokes which covered the letter from top to bottom. The graceful, sweeping *kanji* reminded me of rivers and willow trees and the curving necks of swans. There was only one person who formed their characters so elegantly.

My mother.

I knew instantly that this was the message Hana and I had been waiting for . . .

And now it was in the hands of our enemy.

Chapter 2

I was in silent agony, desperate to launch myself forward and tear the scroll from Uncle's hands. But I knew that I could not draw attention to myself or Hana. To do so would be an act of madness.

Uncle scanned the letter. For a moment he did not react, but then his face flushed a deep, dull red. His hand around the scroll tightened into a fist, crushing the delicate paper.

'Do you know who this is from?' he snapped, glaring at Mister Choji.

Mister Choji shook his head. 'A letter of condolence, perhaps?' he asked. 'The news of Goku's death will have carried across the Province by now.'

'No, it is not a letter of condolence,' Uncle spat. 'This scroll contains words of deceit which condemn Goku as a traitor!'

'A traitor?' Mister Choji echoed, looking astounded. 'What do you mean?'

Uncle sneered. 'It is wise of you to look innocent,' he said. 'Because if I find you have had any part of this plot then I will have you executed.' He shook his clenched fist, crushing the scroll still further. 'This letter is from my treacherous brother's widow. And it is clear that Goku has been helping her.'

I caught a glimpse of the emotions that chased across Mister Choji's face: astonishment, understanding, and finally a loathing of Uncle Hidehira. 'Goku would never behave dishonourably,' he said at last. 'If the Master helped Lord Yoshijiro's widow, then there was a reason for it.'

'Oh, yes. I'm sure there was a reason for it.' Uncle Hidehira's voice was steely. 'This letter mentions Yoshijiro's daughters. The widow is hiding somewhere and she has her son with her, but not the girls. By the gods, if only she had mentioned where they were!'

Uncle Hidehira turned to one of his guards. 'I want a hundred men sent out to search the neighbouring towns and villages for two young female fugitives,' he ordered. 'The men are to turn out every hut and hovel within half a day's ride of the *dojo*. I want those girls found and brought to me.'

Hana clutched my wrist in terror. I put my fingers over hers, hoping to comfort her, but my hand was trembling.

'Yes, Lord,' the guard replied.

'And tell the captain to take twenty men and go to the temple at the foot of Mount Fuji at closing time tomorrow.' A cunning look came over Uncle's face as he scanned the letter again. 'The widow says she will wait for her daughters there, as the sun is setting. Capture her and the boy child and bring them here to me—alive! I want the pleasure of watching them die under *my* sword!'

A chill wind seemed to blow through my soul. Beside me, Hana's lips had turned whiter than paper.

Mister Choji looked angry and shocked. 'Lord, I must protest—' he began.

'Be silent!' Uncle Hidehira snapped. 'You have protested enough. You are not one of my advisers. In fact, I have decided that after today you will be replaced as Master of this *dojo*.'

Mister Choji's mouth tightened. 'My appointment is the wish of the masters and students—' he began.

But Uncle Hidehira interrupted him. 'I don't care about the wishes of the masters and students,' he sneered. 'They will do as they are told! And you're lucky I don't throw you out now—I would, if it wasn't for the funeral. I'm only letting this ceremony go ahead because of my son's foolishness. I have banished Ken-ichi from all my estates, and now I must show the people that I have disowned him.'

I bit my lip. Ken-ichi had been banished. Not only had he left the school and his friends, he had been forced to leave his home and everything that was important to him. For a moment I felt a flicker of compassion for my cousin. But then I reminded myself that Ken-ichi had killed Master Goku. He deserved his banishment.

Uncle suddenly seemed to notice Hana and me for the first time. Hana was staring at him, her horrified gaze fixed on the letter in his hand.

There was a moment of silence, and the scene on the pathway seemed to freeze. Uncle Hidehira stared, black eyes glittering as he took in her blue servant's clothes.

Had he recognized Hana? My heart pounded and I shifted my weight forward onto the balls of my feet, ready to spring forward and help her.

'What are you staring at?' Uncle Hidehira

snarled. He clenched his fists and took a quick step towards Hana, stamping on the path as if to frighten her away. 'Stupid boy. Get out of here! I won't have filthy servant boys listening to matters which are of no concern to them.'

Pale with fear, Hana looked at Mister Choji.

The head servant nodded gently. 'Go,' he said. 'Both of you. There is plenty for you to do to prepare for the funeral.'

As soon as we were out of earshot, I blurted out, 'We must get to Mother and Moriyasu before Uncle's samurai!'

Hana nodded. 'I agree,' she said. 'But please, Kimi, let's stay for the funeral.'

I hesitated. 'But the letter!'

'It doesn't matter if Uncle gets there first, Kimi,' Hana said. 'As long as we are there before the meeting time to stop him.' She paused and I could sense that there was more to her wanting to stay. 'We never got to say goodbye to Father.'

I searched her face and saw that this was something she had to do. I nodded. We would pay our last respects to our Master.

A bell rang out, echoing across the gardens, and signalled that it was almost time for the funeral. Together, Hana and I made our way back to the servants' quarters. Back in our little bedchamber,

Hana and I quickly stripped off our servants' uniforms and changed into formal clothes. We wore short white kimono jackets as was the custom for a funeral, with the wide-legged black *hakama* trousers that all students of the *dojo* wore for formal occasions. Our hair was oiled and tightly tied into boyish top-knots. Our long *nihonto* swords tucked into our sashes.

I put Moriyasu's little bamboo *bokken* beside my sword. 'We won't have time to come back here afterwards.'

Hana took down some black bean and rice cakes from a shelf. She handed several to me and tucked the others into her kimono. 'For the journey,' she said. 'It's a long way to Mount Fuji and we may not find shelter or food.'

Someone tapped on the door frame. I hurried to slide it back, and came face to face with Tatsuya. He gave a sombre bow.

'It's time,' he said simply.

Chapter 3

The three of us entered the practice hall where Goku's body had been kept since he died, and several students in formal dress and a couple of servants were already there, kneeling on small cushions at the centre of the polished wooden floor. They were grouped in a semi-circle around a long open casket which rested on a beautifully lacquered green and gold altar.

One of the servants looked up as we entered the hall. I saw that it was Ko, and beside him knelt another kitchen boy, Sato. Along with Tatsuya, they had been good friends to Hana and me during our time at the *dojo*. It was good that we didn't have to mourn alone.

Over the past three days, I had been focusing on the happy memories: sparring with Goku in the courtyard, learning from him in the scroll room, meditating with him . . .

Goku had been a second father to us—our teacher, our protector; but I had been avoiding visiting his body. I couldn't bear to re-live that terrible moment when the sharp point of the spear had plunged into his chest.

As we approached the casket I caught a glimpse of gleaming wood, a fold of white cotton cloth, and a lotus flower carefully positioned by a pale hand. Beside me, Hana took in a wavering breath.

I looked down into the casket and saw that Master Goku's eyes were closed. His head rested on a small flat pillow and his hands had been placed lightly one on top of the other across the front of a simple white cotton kimono. I felt a quick rush of relief that someone, perhaps Ko or Sato, had honoured tradition and placed a gleaming silver knife across his chest, to keep away the evil spirits.

'He looks as if he's going to sit up and speak to us,' I said softly.

But then I noticed the way his skin was stretched tight over his cheekbones. There was a greenish tinge to his eyelids. His fingers were waxy. Without warning, my vision blurred with tears. Master Goku was dead. Only three days ago, he had been living and breathing. Now he was gone for ever.

Tears streamed down Hana's cheeks as she began to pray. I closed my eyes and tried to clear my mind. But my thoughts wouldn't settle.

Instead, I kept thinking about my father and older brothers, wondering if their spirits would wander, tormented and restless.

I thought of the way Master Goku had taught us to meditate. His deep, calm voice echoed through my head, *Open your mind . . . find the balance . . .*

I took a breath and opened my mind. Memories faded and I could feel Goku's presence somewhere deep within my soul. All at once I realized that he would always be with me. The training he had given me and the lessons he taught were now part of me—just as everything Father had taught me was rooted in me, growing and gathering strength, giving me the skills to one day face Uncle.

I brought myself out of meditation as Mister Choji came into the main hall. He had changed into formal funeral robes, his white hem swishing around his sandalled feet as he crossed the hall.

'This was not how we planned, but a few hours early will not disturb our Master,' Choji said. 'I have notified the village and the temple.'

He paused to bow to the casket, quickly secured the lid in place, and then lifted the lantern down from its stand, ready to lead the procession to the temple. It was a *dojo* tradition to have a lantern lighting the way for the Master's passing and clearly Mister Choji was going to continue the tradition despite the daylight. Usually, the sacred duty of carrying the lantern was reserved for the closest family, but Master Goku had no family, and so his closest friend and fellow teacher would lead the way instead.

His broad face solemn, Mister Choji gestured to us all to rise and lift the casket. The litter was fitted underneath and I felt the smooth wood in my left hand. To my surprise, the casket itself was light, almost weightless, as if most of Goku had already gone. I turned my mind away and tried to focus on the task ahead.

We spaced ourselves evenly, four on each side of the litter, and at a word from Tatsuya who was at the front, we turned and faced the doorway. I noticed a small group of mourners had gathered there, ready to fall in behind us as we proceeded along the pathway to the temple.

Suddenly, I heard an imperious command, and Uncle Hidehira came sweeping in, flanked by a dozen or so of his heavily-armed samurai guards. 'I will lead the procession,' he said abruptly, one hand on the scabbard of his curving sword.

I glanced at Mister Choji. His face turned a dull angry red and there was a moment of tense silence. Then he handed the lantern to Uncle Hidehira and bowed low.

With a satisfied smile, Uncle Hidehira turned to lead the procession out of the hall. As soon as he was out of earshot, I heard Ko, the kitchen boy, speak quietly to Mister Choji. 'It would honour Master Goku if you took my place and helped carry the casket.'

'It is I who is honoured, my son,' Mister Choji said humbly, as Ko gave up his place.

With Uncle Hidehira at the front, we moved slowly out of the main hall and into the morning sunshine. We followed a white pebble pathway and proceeded through the rock gardens, passing lily ponds which reflected the clear blue sky. As we walked, I couldn't help but remember the first time I had seen Master Goku. He had been standing in the gateway of the *dojo*, staring sternly at my cousin Ken-ichi who had challenged me to a duel.

Goku had given us so much. The casket shifted slightly as someone stumbled, and I saw it was Hana. Perhaps she too was thinking about Goku, of his kindness and all the things he had taught us.

At last, the temple came into sight with its tall pagoda building standing near the front of the sacred ground, in a circle of golden gravel. We were headed for the main building with three ornate curving rooftops stacked one above the other. Monks in saffron-yellow robes stood on either side of the steps leading up to the entrance, where a round copper gong hung gracefully from an ash-wood hanger.

The monks bowed their smoothly-shaven heads as Uncle and his guards passed between them and began to climb the steps.

Once my eyes had adjusted to the dimly-lit interior of the temple, I saw an old priest waiting for us by a bronze statue of the Buddha. He had a *shakujo* ritual staff in his hand, the iron rings jingling at the top. Behind him stood an impressive altar, lacquered with green and gold, and touched here and there with glossy black paint.

As we moved forward, the priest rang the altar bell and began to chant, the nasal sound of his words running into each other.

We carefully placed the casket in front of the

altar. Mister Choji nodded his approval and stepped forward to make a final adjustment to its position.

The school filed silently into the temple behind us and kneeled in neat rows. Watched by Uncle Hidehira's samurai guards, the mourners from the nearby villages filled the spaces at the sides of the temple, heads bowed. I could hear a woman quietly weeping near the back. Other mourners had arranged their hair in the traditional samurai style and I guessed they had once been students of Master Goku.

The monks walked slowly up the centre of the temple to continue the ceremony. At the end of the long prayer, the old priest finished chanting and fell silent. There was a moment of peaceful contemplation. I knew that next a relative of the dead should rise and thank the guests for coming. But of course Master Goku had no relative.

I glanced at Mister Choji, wondering whether he would speak, but in my heart I knew it would be Uncle Hidehira. And sure enough, my uncle left his position at the head of Goku's casket and moved forward. I felt a hot rush of hatred for him.

'Friends,' he began in a deep, self-important

voice. 'As well as being *jito* of the southern part of this province, I was Goku's most trusted friend.'

That's not true, I wanted to shout. I saw Mister Choji standing tensely, his face a mask of carefully controlled fury.

'Our friendship began during the days of my training here,' Uncle Hidehira went on, letting his hand rest on the scabbard of his sword. 'Like many of you, I was once a student at the *dojo*. Indeed, Goku once told me that I was the best he had ever seen.' Uncle paused and looked out at the crowd, almost daring someone to challenge that statement. I had to keep my jaw firmly clenched—everyone knew that my father was the best. 'In later years I outstripped his skills and found that I needed a more experienced teacher . . . but I never forgot Goku. And I'm sure you will never forget him either, although you all know it is time to move on.'

Uncle Hidehira paused to let his meaning sink in.

A sob echoed from near the back of the temple. Uncle Hidehira glared, and it was quickly stifled. 'You *must* move on,' he said sharply. 'It is time to go back to your studies. Train hard. Become warriors. Now that I have no son, I will need an heir from among the loyal samurai army that will help build my empire. Goku's death has been an upset for you all, but it was time for a change at this school . . .'

A stir rippled through the students. A few of the older students muttered under their breaths, and I knew they resented Uncle's implication that their Master's time had passed.

'Change is coming,' Uncle Hidehira went on. 'Both to this school and to the Province. I need an army, and as I look at you now I see my future warriors . . . my generals . . . my battle-hungry men. You will train hard and be proud to use your skills in the service of your *jito*.'

As Uncle Hidehira finished his speech, I looked around to see some of the students, their faces alive with excitement. The idea of becoming the *jito*'s heir was surely filling them with purpose. There was a buzz in the air as everyone filed past Goku's casket to bow their last respects. They all bowed to Uncle Hidehira, too, before going out of the doorway at the side of the temple which led to the funeral pyre.

As I watched them, I couldn't help but feel despair. How could they be so taken in by Uncle's words? They were so excited at the thought of using their skills that they couldn't see that most of them were destined for a bloody death on Uncle's battlefields.

We followed the crowd outside to the wide gravel courtyard behind the temple. I caught a glimpse of stone carvings, tall pine trees shading part of the hillside, and a bronze statue of Buddha gleaming in the sunshine.

Even though I had attended my grandmother's funeral many moons ago and knew what to expect, my stomach still tightened when I saw the flaming pyre which had been built in the centre of the courtyard.

There were several large stones, all about the same height and spaced out carefully to support a casket. Between them, the priests had layered dry timber which was flickering fiercely in the breeze. The monks brought Goku's casket and placed it on the broad stones and into the flames.

Sparks flew, some of them spiralling up towards the sky. Silence fell over the assembled crowd. Then one of the monks rang a tinkling bell and began to chant. Soon the others joined in, their voices blending into a gentle melody.

As the fire began to consume the casket, I felt tears welling up. So many people I had loved were gone! My father, my brothers, and now Master Goku . . .

I tried to blink the tears away; I tried to control my grief. But it was no good. The tears fell, hot against my skin.

I felt Hana move closer to me, and I reached sideways to touch her fingers with mine. Around us, the chanting of the monks rose and fell.

Above us, the sun climbed higher in the sky, beating down on our heads. An incredible heat filled the courtyard as the pyre became a furnace, making the air ripple and shimmer, until at last the casket disappeared into a raging inferno of heat and flame.

When the fire subsided, the priest stepped forward and raked the pyre carefully with a long metal pole.

Soon, the last remains of Master Goku were revealed. White bones gleamed among the smouldering embers. Most were still recognizable for what they were—long shins, round hipbones, a smooth skull.

A monk brought out a large urn wrapped in pure white cloth. He removed the cloth and stood quietly beside the pyre. A second monk brought two pairs of fine chopsticks. He gave one pair to Uncle Hidehira and the other to Mister Choji.

I watched as Uncle reached into the pyre and carefully selected a bone from one of Master

Goku's feet. As tradition demanded, he held it out to Mister Choji, who solemnly accepted the bone between his own chopsticks.

Mister Choji carefully placed the pure white bone into the bottom of the urn. He turned and beckoned to the nearest casket-bearer. I knew that each of us in turn would approach the funeral pyre and accept one of Master Goku's bones from Uncle Hidehira in this way. We would place them in the urn, beginning with the feet and working all the way up the skeleton until the last mourner placed Master Goku's skull in the urn. My mother had once explained that custom demanded the dead be placed in an urn the right way up, so they could be comfortable in their final resting place.

When it was my turn, I kept my head bowed, hoping Uncle wouldn't look at me too closely. When I took the chopsticks, Uncle Hidehira barely looked at me as he passed me a small shining white bone. He seemed to hurry through the motions, wanting to be anywhere but here. Carefully, I took the bone between my own chopsticks. Heart pounding, I placed the bone in the urn on top of the other pieces.

Immediately, the old priest stepped forward. He was holding a large piece of stone carved into the shape of a long-stemmed mushroom. He placed this in the urn and began to rock it back and forth. I heard a brittle cracking sound and guessed the priest was crushing the bones.

I turned and passed the chopsticks to Hana. She glanced up at me, her eyes huge with sorrow. Her hand trembled slightly as she took the chopsticks and I knew that this ceremony was especially hard on her. In the same way that the priest was crushing the bones to make them fit into the urn, so my sister and I had to crush our emotions so that we would not falter in the face of the terrible events which had overtaken us.

Hana took the chopsticks and gave me the tiniest nod as I passed her on my way back to my place. As I turned, I was filled with pride that her hand was steady as she received the next bone.

Above us, a single bird of prey wheeled and circled.

At last, the priest used the carved stone to crush the round skull bones. Then the urn was wrapped neatly in a white cloth and presented to Uncle Hidehira, who led the way back inside the temple.

We proceeded behind him, our steps slow and respectful. I felt relief that Goku's spirit would be happy here, near the *dojo* he loved so much, and knew that Hana and I could set out on our journey knowing he was at peace.

All the mourners gathered inside the temple for the final moments of the funeral. At last, Uncle placed the urn on the altar and after a pause it was time for the mourners to file past, one by one, to head back to the *dojo*. The casket-bearers were to go first, offer a formal bow to Goku's casket and then the *jito* before moving towards the front temple doors.

When it came to my turn, I had to steel myself to keep my head down and bow to Uncle Hidehira, pretending to offer my respect.

Mister Choji was behind me. As I moved forward, following Hana and Tatsuya, I glanced back over my shoulder and saw Master Choji approach the altar and bow respectfully to the urn rather than to the *jito*. He paused in front of Uncle Hidehira. But he did not bow as we had done. He simply stared at Uncle, his chin tilted up defiantly.

I could see Uncle Hidehira's cheeks flushing slightly as he met Mister Choji's gaze. There was a moment of silence in the temple, as if everyone present was holding their breath.

I bit my lip, knowing that this was a deliberate act of defiance from Mister Choji. He had suffered Uncle's insults in silence all morning, holding himself tightly in check. But now he had had enough.

He deliberately turned away from the *jito*, his head held high.

A spasm of rage passed over Uncle Hidehira's face and I watched in shock as his sword was drawn. The long blade flashed upwards, then came slicing down across Mister Choji's body.

His blood spurted in a wide arc.

Chapter 4

With a look of savage triumph, Uncle Hidehira drew his sword back, shook Mister Choji's blood from the blade, and re-sheathed it.

Mister Choji staggered. His face was desperate as he reached for something to steady himself against. His fingers found the edge of the altar and for one horrifying moment I thought that he would knock into the urn of bones and send it crashing to the floor.

The crowd behind us gasped in horror as Mister Choji toppled forward, eyes glazed. His body hit the floor with a dull thud. The monks looked shocked, but none dared to speak out against the *jito*.

Rage swelled up inside me as chaos broke out all around. Some of the students rushed to Mister Choji's side, while the mourners cried out in agony for the disturbed peace of Master Goku's spirit.

'He is heartless,' Hana murmured, her face ashen.

Beside me, Tatsuya's eyes darkened with menace as his gaze shifted from Choji's body to Uncle Hidehira and his right hand went instinctively to the hilt of his sword.

I saw my friend Ko, the kitchen boy, on his knees, cradling Mister Choji's head. 'How could you?' Ko shouted at Uncle. 'How could you?'

One of the older boys shouted, 'Murder!' as he jostled through the crowded temple in Uncle Hidehira's direction.

There was a whisper of cold steel as Uncle's guards unsheathed their swords. Several of the village mourners cried out and fled from the temple.

In two strides Tatsuya covered the distance between himself and Uncle Hidehira, joining the older student with his sword in his hand. At once six of the samurai guards moved into defensive positions around the *jito*. Their eyes were glittering and watchful.

'You killed him,' Tatsuya said. 'Why?'

'Because I am Lord Steward and my word is law,' Uncle Hidehira snarled, his eyes narrowing as he glared at Tatsuya, from within his protected circle. 'You would do well to remember that your loyalty is bound to me, boy.'

Tatsuya stared at Uncle, and I could see he was torn. Did his loyalty belong to the *jito*? Or to the Master?

'You may be the *jito*,' he cried, 'but you have shed blood in a holy place! And at the funeral of our Master!'

My spirit soared at his words. Not everyone was willing to bow beneath Uncle's cruelty. My fingers tingled, ready to draw a weapon. Had the time come for me to face my father's murderer? To challenge him honourably in battle? Was I ready for it?

I drew my sword and stepped forward, steeling myself. 'Not only that!' I exclaimed, no longer caring that Uncle might recognize me. 'You've robbed us of our *new* Master, a man we knew and respected.'

Uncle Hidehira sneered at the sword in my hand. 'Those who draw a sword against their *jito* are traitors,' he said. 'Just as your Masters were both traitors.' He glanced at the urn on the altar.

'Goku's bones will have the final resting place he deserves—scattered beneath the feet of my conquering army.'

Such an act would mean eternal torment for Goku's soul.

'Goku and Choji were not traitors!' I cried. 'They were loyal to the true *jito*, the honourable Yamamoto no Yoshijiro!'

My rage drove me forward in a sudden lunge, but two of Uncle's samurai guards shoved me back into the knot of boys that had gathered behind Tatsuya and me. I caught a glimpse of Hana, beside me. Her eyes were full of grim determination.

All around me, students were coming together. Rebellion and defiance rippled through the air. Ko leapt to his feet beside Mister Choji. 'Master Goku was no traitor!' he cried.

'Nor was Mister Choji!' Sato muttered through gritted teeth.

The time is now! my soul cried out. *We must have vengeance for the deaths of our father and older brothers . . .*

I had to get through the samurai to Uncle. I flexed my knees and held my sword in a two-handed grip. The hilt felt smooth and familiar in my hand, the steel perfectly balanced. I fixed my gaze on Uncle Hidehira, vengeance burning in the pit of my belly and launched my attack.

Hardened warriors used to battle, the samurai disbanded from their protective circle and leaped forward to protect their master.

'Kill the traitors!' shouted Uncle.

Suddenly, all around me, students were battling with Uncle Hidehira's guards.

A blade came slicing down near my head. I deflected it and twisted around to meet another attack. I caught sight of the priest as he darted forward into the fray, his aged face etched with horror. 'Stop!' he cried, waving his hands. 'Violence is forbidden in this holy place . . . '

But no one listened. Students pushed past him as they sprang to defend their friends. My samurai enemy fought with determination, but my focus was on getting past him to Uncle. Tatsuya swept into my field of vision, whirling his blade as he fought at my left side. Hana was on my right, her sword glittering.

Although there were fewer than twenty of Uncle's guards, it seemed as though there were hundreds. They moved so fast, fought so skilfully, their blades slicing. But the students worked together against the experienced soldiers, and my heart soared with hope.

Several students hovered in the doorway to the temple, away from the fighting. I recognized two of them as friends of my cousin Ken-ichi, their faces pale with fright, looking as if they might run away at any moment.

They're cowards, I thought, as I twisted around to attack again the samurai I was fighting.

Behind him, I saw Uncle Hidehira calmly slice his sword downwards, striking a nearby student across the wrist and severing his hand. The boy cried out and fell to his knees, blood soaking through the sleeve of his kimono, another innocent claimed by Uncle's blade. A second student yelled furiously and leapt at the *jito*, elbows bent and sword held high. But Uncle Hidehira defended easily, cutting the boy down with a swift slashing movement. Uncle's speed was breathtaking; his skill comparable to that of my father or Master Goku.

As I fought my way towards him, I wondered if anyone could match him. Was I ready? I wasn't certain, but this was my moment to try. I would avenge my father and brothers, my master and my friends—even if it killed me!

'*Haaai!*' Another samurai leapt in front of me, arcing his sword down towards my shoulder. His red silk *mon* badge was like a slash of blood against his armour.

I kept myself centred as I stepped just out of range of his strike. I moved in to attack, but the samurai recovered. He lunged again. I bent my knees and then powered upwards, pushing through my thighs to attack him with my sword, hard and fast. He blocked me and brought his other arm in from the side, grabbing my wrist and pressing hard with his thumb . . . and suddenly my grip on the hilt was loosened. My sword went clattering to the ground.

I found myself empty-handed and defenceless, and a look of triumph flickered across the samurai's battle-hardened face.

'Weep, child, for you are defeated,' he snarled, and abruptly flung his sword up high.

Death was coming for me and I had not even had a chance to challenge my uncle.

But suddenly something buzzed past my shoulder, skimming my cheek. The samurai let out a shriek of pain. He dropped his sword and clutched at his face. Blood poured down his cheeks as he fell to his knees, still shrieking. Had someone thrown a knife? I glanced at the floor, my gaze attracted by a flash of silver.

It was a steel hairpin that I could see protruding

from between the hands of the writhing samurai. I had seen that hairpin only this morning, when Hana had fastened her top-knot . . .

Twisting around fast, I saw that Hana was ten paces away from me. Her hand was poised at shoulder height, from where she had thrown the pin.

Without the hairpin her long hair had come loose, flowing down to her waist like a cloak of rippling black silk. Our eyes locked and sudden realization seemed to lance through Hana's mind. It would be clear to anyone who looked that she was a girl.

For a frozen moment Hana stood motionless. Then she dropped her sword and reached for her long hair, scooping it up, desperately trying to twist its rippling length back into a top-knot.

I had to help her before anyone saw!

I grabbed up my sword and dashed through the chaos towards my sister. Another samurai reared up in front of me, snarling like a mad dog. I leapt to the side and pushed all my strength through my right leg to deliver a hard-edged kick to his chest.

The samurai staggered backwards and I ran on, ducking beneath a sword on my left, a short spear on my right. Power hummed through my limbs. My ears rang with the clashes of metal around me.

I reached Hana just as a roar ripped the air above our heads.

'Traitor!' shouted my uncle Hidehira.

Breathless, I turned to see that he was pointing at Hana. His face was a mask of rage. His narrow eyes glittered dangerously.

'Seize that girl!' he bellowed.

Chapter 5

Shock rippled through the temple as monks and samurai looked in the direction Uncle Hidehira was pointing. Several students gaped at Hana's waist-length hair.

'A girl?' someone gasped. 'But who is she?'

'Her name is Yamamoto no Hana,' roared Uncle Hidehira. 'And she is a traitor!'

I caught a glimpse of Ko, gaping in shock. Beside him, Sato recovered quickly from his surprise. His face broke into a gleeful grin.

Just then, Uncle Hidehira's glance flickered to me. Recognition washed across his hard features, swiftly followed by triumph. 'Standing beside

Hana is her elder sister, Kimi. They are fugitives; seize them now!'

The priest gasped. 'They are the daughters of the old *jito*!'

Now everyone knew who we were, and the threat we could represent to Uncle.

Hana reached out and touched my fingers gently, gripping her sword in her other hand. Like our older brothers who had perished before us, we would fight to the death rather than be taken by Uncle Hidehira and his men.

The last of the mourners hurried out of the temple at the threat of more bloodshed.

Hana and I stood shoulder to shoulder, weapons raised. A tight formation of Uncle Hidehira's soldiers moved towards us from the front. I slid my right foot back and centred myself. We were ready to face them.

But suddenly there were more behind us! I had no time to act defensively before I felt a strong arm wrap around me to pin my arms to my sides, my sword dangling uselessly.

I struggled wildly.

'Keep still,' grunted the samurai who held me captive, and I felt the cold sharp kiss of a *tanto* dagger at my throat. 'One move and I slit your throat.'

My hope faded.

Beside me, Hana was also being held by one of Uncle's men with the tip of a knife pricked beneath her chin. We were doomed.

From the corner of my eye, I caught a glimpse of Tatsuya. He was standing in front of Uncle Hidehira, legs braced as he held his sword in an attack position—a two-handed grip, elbows high and sword-tip pointing to the ceiling. A group of other students and servants were grouped around him like a small army. I saw Ko, his dark eyes fierce. Next to him was Sato. He had snatched up a long-handled brass staff and was holding it like a *jo*.

'Your guards are all over there,' Tatsuya said loudly to Uncle, nodding his head in our direction. 'Which leaves you alone and outnumbered, Lord Steward.'

I saw Hana watching Tatsuya with admiration. I felt proud that he was our friend.

'Do you think you are better than me, little boy? Attack me if you dare,' Uncle Hidehira said coldly. He swept the assembled students with a piercing glare. 'Which of you will be first to die on my blade?'

A few of the students cast doubtful looks at

each other, but Tatsuya, Ko, and Sato held their positions.

Uncle Hidehira sneered. 'Traitors,' he said. 'Death is coming for you . . . and you . . . and you . . . ' The students flinched as he jabbed his sword at each of them in turn. 'If you survive today you'll be executed for daring to attack your lord! Do you want to heap that shame upon your families?'

There was a moment's hesitation. One of the students met my gaze and looked away in shame. Then they lowered their weapons and backed away, their bravado gone.

'Get out of my sight,' Uncle Hidehira barked and sheathed his sword. The students fled, but Tatsuya, Ko, and Sato did not move.

I watched them disappear through the doorway of the temple, my heart aching. But I couldn't blame them for running away. It was no easy thing to rebel against a *jito*.

Uncle Hidehira stood motionless, his right hand rested dangerously on his scabbard hilt, ready to draw in the blink of an eye. He stared at Tatsuya, daring him to attack. Our friend gazed back at him coolly. I knew that if Hana and I were to have any chance, we had to break free now, while Uncle's attention was on Tatsuya.

I glanced at Hana. She gave a sharp nod. Hana let out a yell and twisted free from her captor. Immediately, I jabbed my elbow into the gut of the soldier who was holding me. As he bent double with pain, I reached up and seized the arm he was using to hold me. With a sharp, swift movement, I stepped backwards and then wielded his arm like a sword using his own weight to throw him into another samurai who had realized what I was doing and was leaping forward to attack.

'Don't let them escape, you fools!' bellowed Uncle Hidehira furiously.

Tatsuya, Ko, and Sato cast us startled glances, but almost immediately Ko leaped across the room with a wild yell. He unleashed a fierce side kick that took the nearest samurai by surprise and sent him flying.

'Run!' Sato yelled at Hana and me, as he fought two samurai at once. 'Run, both of you, while you have the chance!'

Uncle Hidehira let out a terrifying battle cry and slashed his sword at Tatsuya, who evaded him by spinning away. Tatsuya swept his own blade upwards and brought it down in a hard diagonal slice. There was a clash of steel on steel as Uncle Hidehira blocked him.

'Run!' Tatsuya yelled.

I hesitated, torn between the need to stay and fight with my friends and the instinct to flee. But the thought of Uncle's samurai riding to Mount Fuji to capture my mother pulled me away.

Hana seized my arm. 'Come on!' she cried. We thrust our swords back into our scabbards and together we ducked under the clawing hands of Uncle's samurai, racing across the temple. As we passed the altar, I caught sight of the urn, wrapped in white cloth. My heart ached at the thought of Master Goku's bones being crushed beneath the feet of Uncle Hidehira's army. I couldn't leave the *sensei's* remains there.

My hand shot out and I grabbed the urn. Cradling it in my arm, I raced with Hana to the doorway of the temple. Outside, we took the steps at a flying run, dashing past horror-stuck monks. The sun was in our eyes and Hana flung up one hand, dazzled.

A shout went up behind us. 'After the girls!' Uncle Hidehira roared.

'This way!' I said, praying that Tatsuya would not fall by my uncle's hand. I hurtled across the gravel path towards the forest. Hana was at my heels. Tiny stones crunched beneath our feet. Shadows closed around us as the trees blocked out the sunshine.

I could hear a group of samurai crashing after us as we plunged through the undergrowth. We varied our course—moving left, then right, then, left again. I gripped the urn tightly in the curve of my arm, my hand wrapped around it. My sword in its scabbard beat against my leg.

Behind us, Uncle Hidehira bellowed like an angry bull. He must have come out of the temple to stand at the top of the steps, because his voice now echoed loudly through the forest. 'Bring them down,' he yelled, 'but do not kill them! Bring them back to me alive!'

'Run faster, Kimi,' Hana urged breathlessly.

She grabbed my hand and held it tight. Together we leaped over tangled undergrowth and darted around trees. Branches whipped at our faces. Coarse grass slashed our feet. As we went deeper into the heart of the forest, shadows loomed on either side and the scent of pine was strong.

Uncle's voice faded, but his samurai were so close behind us that I could hear the banging of their armour and weapons. How many of them were there—six, ten? Hoarse voices shouted commands: 'Over there!' and 'Split up . . . go left!'

Hana and I went right, curving away from the

samurai. I could hear them crashing away to our left.

But we were getting away! We broke out of the trees and into a clearing on the hillside, a grassy glade dappled with sunlight.

My breath rasped hot in my chest and my mind plunged this way and that. What should we do— keep going? Or try to hide and pray that the samurai kept on going, chasing shadows through the forest?

Insects buzzed in the still air. A dead branch snapped behind us, too close, and I knew then that someone was coming. Fear lanced through me.

'There's nowhere to hide,' I whispered to Hana.

'We must go on,' she whispered back, a determined look on her face. 'We can't let them capture us, Kimi, or there will be no one to warn Mother and Moriyasu about Uncle's trap!'

If we didn't get to Mount Fuji, all hope would be lost. I clutched the urn tighter. It was so bulky. As we launched ourselves across the clearing, I risked a glance back over my shoulder.

One of Uncle Hidehira's samurai soldiers was rushing up behind us; his face was hard as steel, his dark eyes full of murder.

'No!' I yelped, and plunged forward, grabbing Hana and taking her with me.

We hurtled across the glade towards a weeping willow tree on the far side. Beyond its drooping branches, I could see an open pathway, snaking through the trees, heading down the hillside. Hana and I could run fast, maybe even out-run the samurai in his heavy armour.

But just as hope began to soar, I caught a glimpse of something large and dark breaking from the shadows to my left. A second samurai! And there a third!

Quickly Hana and I veered right, away from them. At once, another soldier came racing in towards us from that side, too. We were pinned on three sides . . .

I curved back to the left, dragging my sister along with me. I fixed my gaze on the willow tree and the promise of that clear path. We had to get there. We must! We had one last chance—get beyond the willow and run for our lives.

But up ahead, two more samurai stepped out from behind the drooping branches of the willow. The long curving horns on their iron helmets caught a shaft of sunlight which slanted down through the trees as they barred the way.

We stopped running then, trapped, outnumbered. I could hear the six samurai breathing hard, and the creak of their leather armour as they moved in closer. Closer . . . Closer . . . So close I could smell them—their sweat, the stinking grease they used under their armour to keep lice at bay.

I let the urn in its white cloth wrapping slip down my body, rolling it gently until it rested in the long grass at my feet. Six pairs of samurai eyes were fixed on my face.

'No tricks, girl,' muttered their leader. 'Give yourself up quietly, and the *jito* may show you mercy . . .'

'The *jito* knows no mercy,' I replied, stepping forward away from the urn. Hana and I unsheathed our swords in the same breath.

Steel whispered in the clean bright air as we took a firm stance. We held our weapons ready. Hana shook her long hair back. Her face was determined.

My heart slowed and I felt power humming through my limbs.

There was a moment of silence. Peace settled on the grassy glade. Then all six samurai were upon us, yelling wildly, whirling their swords around their heads as they unleashed a storming attack. Sunlight flashed on steel as I deflected first one blow and then the next. Beside me Hana knocked away a third.

I sliced my sword wide to the right and brought it back fast, dancing on the tips of my toes as I slashed upwards, then down, meeting an attacking blade with every movement. My heart raced.

'Haiii!' The fearsome yells of the six samurai filled our ears as the men attacked.

One of the samurai swept low with his sword, aiming for my ankles. I leaped up over his blade, slashing my own *nihonto* across his stomach. The resistance of his hard leather armour saved his life, but my sword sliced a deep gash in it. I caught a glimpse of red blood—he was wounded! But there was no time for triumph because the samurai came right back at me, eyes flashing like a demon. Our blades crossed and twisted as I put up a high block.

From the corner of my eye I glimpsed Hana, buckling under the onslaught of two samurai blades, and I knew the situation was turning against us. We would be captured and taken to Uncle—and he would dispatch us both, grinning with triumph.

As my thoughts distracted me, the samurai I was fighting ducked under my attack and rushed, grabbing me by the neck. I couldn't breathe.

Blood roared in my ears and black spots danced across my vision.

Mother! I cried silently, my heart aching, for there would be no one to warn her now.

Suddenly a loud battle cry tore the air and something flashed near my head.

An arrow! It buried itself in a narrow gap in the samurai's armour, where shoulder-guard met breast-plate.

Releasing his grip on my throat, the samurai howled and staggered backwards. Without hesitation, I recovered my balance and plunged my sword quickly into the opening I had already made in his armour, opening his stomach with a spurt of blood.

As the samurai fell to the ground, I swung round to see where the arrow had come from.

Chapter 6

Tatsuya came bursting out of the shadows at the edge of the glade, a longbow in his hand and a handful of arrows bristling in his sash. He must have snatched it from one of Uncle's guards!

Even as he ran, Tatsuya was fitting another arrow to the string and drawing back.

With a savage yell, he loosed a second arrow and then a third.

The shafts flickered through the air. I ducked, and one arrow flew above my head to hit a second of the samurai soldiers, one that was fighting Hana. Its lethal tip pierced his throat.

The samurai's eyes bulged. His mouth opened in

a silent scream. Then he pitched forward and fell face down at Hana's feet. The next arrow took a slice from a third samurai's cheek, and the next came flying low to bury itself in another samurai's thigh.

Two men were dead and another two wounded, with two more left to fight.

'I couldn't land a single blow,' Tatsuya said, breathless, and I knew he meant against Uncle.

'But you escaped,' Hana replied, as the samurai recovered and began to attack.

Tatsuya was out of arrows. With a muttered curse, he tossed the longbow into the grass and drew his sword. He leapt at the samurai with the wounded cheek, blade held high, bringing it around in a swinging cut as if he would slice the man's head from his shoulders. The warrior stepped sideways to avoid Tatsuya's strike, but as he half-turned, he accidentally opened himself up to me.

I struck hard, putting all my power through my sword arm. My blade slashed cleanly through the gap between two plates of armour. The samurai gasped for breath and dropped to his knees, dying.

One of the others came in fast from my left, blade raised above his head. I quickly blocked and as our blades clashed, blood smeared on the steel.

I braced myself, dropped my shoulder, and shoved hard. The samurai staggered backwards. Behind him, Tatsuya pulled back the man's helmet. The hilt of his sword flashed up into the man's temple, knocking him unconscious.

Only two samurai remained, but one was badly injured by the arrow in his leg and I knew we could defeat them now. Hana was fighting hard, her sword flashing as she slashed and swiped. Her opponent was a tall man, a powerful fighter who had so far avoided being wounded, and he was driving my sister backwards.

Swiftly, Hana pivoted, and as the samurai's momentum carried him forward, she stepped in behind him. He was startled as she simply placed one hand on his shoulder, and pulled him backwards and down. He toppled easily, and she turned again, slicing across him with her blade.

Hana's face was turned away and all I could see was the curve of one pale cheek half-hidden by a halo of black hair, as the samurai let out his last cry.

And then there were no more samurai left to fight. Bodies lay all around and insects hummed in the air around my face.

The only movement was from the samurai with Tatsuya's arrow in his thigh. With a bellow of pain, he pulled the shaft out, then staggered to his feet and half ran, half limped across the glade away from us.

When he reached the tree line, he turned and snarled, 'There is no escape from the *jito*. Lord Hidehira will track you down and kill you!' Then he vanished into the shadows.

'I'm trembling,' Hana whispered, holding out a shaking hand.

I looked at my sister, then grabbed her into a fierce hug. 'We've escaped, Hana,' I said.

Then I turned to Tatsuya. 'I don't know how to thank you.'

'You saved our lives, Tatsuya,' Hana put in, her face glowing as she looked up at him.

Tatsuya slipped his sword back into its scabbard and gave a little bow. 'You don't need to thank me,' he said. 'We're friends. More than friends!' He clasped his fist in front of his chest and bowed his head for a moment. 'I pledge you my loyalty for as long as it takes for you to restore honour and goodness to the title of *jito* of these estates.'

The image of Tatsuya crossing swords with Uncle flashed in my mind. 'But how did you get away?' I asked.

Tatsuya looked triumphant. 'Ko and Sato took

down two of the soldiers and escaped out of the back of the temple.'

'But you were fighting Uncle,' Hana said.

Tatsuya grinned. He pulled his kimono away from his body and showed us a shallow, thin cut across his stomach. 'He wasn't quick enough to finish me off. I broke away as soon as I could to come and find you.'

'Thank you, Tatsuya,' Hana said gravely. She picked up his discarded longbow and handed it to him ceremoniously.

'We should get out of here,' I said, sheathing my sword and hurrying to retrieve Master Goku's urn from the long grass. 'As soon as Uncle hears we've escaped, he'll send more troops after us.'

Hana nodded. 'And we have to hurry if we're to get to Mount Fuji before sunset tomorrow.'

'Mount Fuji? Why do you want to go there?' Tatsuya stood up, looking at us expectantly.

'Our mother has been sending letters to Master Goku,' Hana began. 'We didn't tell you before because we thought it would be safer if no one else knew about it.'

Tatsuya frowned. 'But . . . I could have helped.'

Hana stepped forward and touched Tatsuya lightly on the arm. 'We know that now,' Hana said, smiling gently.

Tatsuya looked into Hana's eyes, and I knew he understood. It would be sad to say goodbye to such a true friend.

'Tell me about the letters,' Tatsuya said.

'Seven scrolls came in the weeks before the tournament,' Hana explained. 'But Master Goku kept them from us. He wanted us to stay at the *dojo* where he could keep us safe.'

Quickly, she told him how another letter had arrived that morning, and that Uncle had learned Mother wanted to meet us in the temple at the foot of Mount Fuji. Tatsuya listened closely.

'Uncle Hidehira dispatched soldiers immediately,' Hana went on. 'He's setting a trap to capture Mother and Moriyasu!'

Tatsuya nodded. 'And you're going there to warn them.'

'We have to get to Mount Fuji before the meeting time and intercept them.' I glanced up at the sun, burning high above. 'We have the rest of today, and then tomorrow until sundown.'

'A day and a half for travelling,' Hana said slowly. 'Is that enough?'

'Maybe,' Tatsuya said. He frowned thoughtfully, as if calculating the journey in his head. 'At a guess, I'd say Mount Fuji is two days away. But if we hurry, we can make it in time.'

'*We?*' I stared at him, my heart suddenly light as air. 'You're coming with us?'

'There's nothing for me back at the *dojo*, now,' Tatsuya said. He clenched his fist and held it out in front of him. 'And I've made a pledge, remember? We're in this together. Loyal friends!'

Hana and I exchanged a glance. Then we clenched our own fists and placed them over Tatsuya's, one on top of the other. 'Loyal friends!' we chorused.

Quickly, we gathered up weapons from the dead and unconscious samurai. One samurai had an empty leather rice pouch, which I relieved him of. Instead of carrying the heavy urn, I carefully emptied its contents into the thick, waterproof pouch and tied it to my sash. I knew Goku would not be offended by the action. I would take him somewhere he could find peace.

Tatsuya watched me, his face grave. 'You did the right thing taking the urn,' he said quietly. 'Master Goku deserves a sacred resting place.'

I nodded. 'I thought we might find somewhere when we reach Mount Fuji,' I said.

'That's a wonderful idea, Kimi,' Hana said warmly. 'Father always said it was one of the most beautiful, peaceful places on earth.'

'Mount Fuji was special to Master Goku, too,'

Tatsuya said, kneeling over one of the dead soldiers. He was unstrapping a quiver of arrows from the man's back, but he paused and glanced up at Hana. 'He was born near there. Sometimes during lessons he would refer to the mountain as the soul of the kingdom.'

'Then it's right that it should be his final resting place,' Hana replied. 'We should take his ashes to the temple where we're to meet Mother.'

I nodded. 'Master Goku's spirit will draw strength from being in such a sacred and special resting place.'

Tatsuya fastened his quiver of arrows to his sash.

We left the glade in single file, Tatsuya taking the lead as we hurried along the pathway through the forest. Hana was ahead of me. She'd left her hair down, loose to her waist, its blue-black sheen the colour of a raven's wing. I had decided to keep mine up like a boy. It wasn't so important to keep up our disguises now because Uncle Hidehira knew who we were, but I found it more comfortable to keep my hair out of my eyes.

Tatsuya set a good pace. The forest closed in around us, shadowy and mysterious. The only sound was the whisper of grass against our ankles.

Every so often we would stop and strain our ears for the creak of leather armour, the rattle of weapons following us. But there was nothing to hear except the distant shriek and chatter of a monkey, the buzz of insects, and the occasional shrill cry of a bird.

Soon we broke out of the forest and found ourselves on a hillside overlooking a wide green valley. Farmers in flat straw hats paddled through the shallow water that flooded the rice fields. In the distance an enormous snow-capped mountain rose up from a crest of pine trees, its foothills wreathed in lilac shadows.

'Mount Fuji,' Hana said in a breathless voice.

Drinking in the sight, I felt anticipation whisper through my soul. This time tomorrow, we would be at the temple, reunited with Mother. Smiling, I put my hand to my waist and touched the hilt of Moriyasu's little bamboo *bokken*.

'Your uncle is sure to send out samurai to hunt us down,' Tatsuya said, eyeing the farmers down in the fields. 'It would be safer for these people if they didn't see us.'

Hana nodded. 'We'll keep off the main paths.'

We cut around the edge of the valley, keeping Mount Fuji ahead of us, fixed in our sights like a talisman. Time passed and the sun slid sideways

73

across the sky, its golden light shimmering on the flooded rice fields.

We picked our way along a narrow track that cut across the hillside. As I followed the others, I glanced out across the peaceful landscape, trying to imagine war-bands riding hard across the horizon with the sun glinting from their helmets. What would the country look like, several moons from now? The people would be starving, all their rice seized to feed the army. There would only be girl-children left to tend the meagre crops because the boys would be rounded up and sent to train as warriors and foot-soldiers.

Suddenly I heard a rustling sound away to my left. Someone was coming towards us through the bamboo!

'Get off the path!' I hissed to the others.

We dived into the undergrowth on the other side of the path, pressing ourselves flat to the ground. The rustling grew louder. I exchanged a panicked look with the others. Was this the advance guard of a foot patrol of soldiers sent by Uncle Hidehira to scour the countryside? My heart was pounding so loudly I was sure that whoever was coming must be able to hear it.

Abruptly a footstep crunched onto the narrow

track, and then another. I heard someone take a wheezing breath.

I peered through the undergrowth. If someone was coming for us, I wanted to see them first! Beside me, Hana reached for the hilt of her sword. Tatsuya was tense and ready.

The footsteps crunched closer and closer . . . and an old woodcutter came into view. He had a lined, leathery face. A basket of pine logs was strapped to his shoulders.

We let the old man make his way along the path, and waited until he had disappeared from view before we scrambled to our feet and brushed ourselves down.

'Well done, Kimi,' Hana said to me.

Tatsuya nodded. 'Your ears are sharp,' he said approvingly. 'No one's going to sneak up on us and get away with it.'

I grinned and we went on our way, pressing along the track that wound towards Mount Fuji.

Later we passed a hot spring, bubbling up out of the ground and filling the air with clouds of steam. We stopped for a moment and sat on a rock to rest our feet while we shared our black bean and rice cakes. Looking around, I noticed that the ground had become steadily inclined and rockier.

After we had eaten, I tilted my face up towards

the sun, enjoying the feel of its warmth on my face. So much had happened today: despair, hope, and finally fear as we battled for our lives in the grassy glade. Exhausted, I tried to draw a veil over my mind and let the peace of the afternoon envelop me.

Tatsuya crouched some distance away, his bow held loosely in his hands as he gazed around at the rocks and sparse trees which surrounded the hot spring. Beyond him to the north was the sapphire gleam of one of the *Fujigoko*, the collection of five lakes at the foot of Mount Fuji.

Hana went to kneel by the edge of the spring and trailed her fingers in the warm water. 'It's like a bath,' she said, smiling. 'The water must have come from deep underground, heated up by the fiery volcano beneath Mount Fuji . . . '

Her voice trailed off as we both noticed that Tatsuya was staring into the distance, eyes narrowed and body tense.

'What is it?' I asked, dropping my voice to a whisper.

'There's someone watching us,' Tatsuya murmured. He slid his gaze away, scanning the hillside.

My stomach tightened. 'Where?' I asked, glancing around.

'Over there.' He jerked his chin in the direction of a flat rock. 'Don't make it obvious that you're looking. It would be better if whoever it is thought we hadn't spotted them.'

Keeping my head still, I swivelled my eyes to the left, following the line of our pathway which curved and twisted through the foothills of Mount Fuji. Far ahead, I could just make out a small dark shape, half-hidden behind a rock. My heart began to hammer.

'Do you think it's one of Uncle's men?' I asked.

I noticed that Tatsuya had reached down and was slipping an arrow from where he'd fastened them to his sash. 'I think it's someone far worse than Lord Hidehira's men,' he said quietly.

'What do you mean?' I asked.

Tatsuya didn't answer at first, but instead let his longbow slip from his shoulder. Stealthily, he fitted his arrow to the string.

When he spoke his next word, a shard of icy fear plunged into my soul.

'*Ninja!*'

Chapter 7

Ninja were the one thing my father feared.

Unlike a samurai, who was bound by the honour of the *bushi* code, a ninja obeyed his own rules. Stealthy and cunning, he could creep up to a man and kill him instantly, or slay him from a distance with a deadly poisoned dart. He was a murderer for hire.

'What should we do?' Hana asked Tatsuya.

'Let's go back and find another pathway.' Tatsuya began to turn round, but I stopped him.

'We haven't got time,' I said. 'We must be at the temple by sundown tomorrow.'

Tatsuya's jaw tightened. 'But we could be walking into a trap.'

Hana looked back and forth between us, considering. 'There are three of us and only one of him.'

Tatsuya glanced at the distant figure half-hidden behind the rock. 'There may be only one of him,' he said. 'But he'll have the strength of three men and the skill of ten.'

'It could take hours to find another path. We have to go this way,' I insisted.

'All right,' Tatsuya said, reluctantly. 'But we must be prepared for anything.'

We made our way cautiously along the steep path. There was only enough room for us to go single file. Tatsuya insisted on going first, holding his longbow hidden behind him. I followed him, my hand on the scabbard of my sword, and Hana brought up the rear, trying to look casual and unconcerned.

Up ahead, the ninja stayed motionless. The thought of him watching us sent a chill along my spine.

The ninja were such a secretive organization, mysterious shadow-warriors, highly skilled and stealthy. My elder brother Harumasa had been fascinated by the stories and legends that people told about them: they could walk through walls, fade into the shadows, even fly.

Harumasa had told me many legends about the first ninja, but my favourite story was that a corrupt monk had murdered a man in cold blood, and the man's young son swore revenge. The son waited and watched his enemy for many moons. One night, when the monk was sleeping beside a burning lantern, moths swarmed in through the open bamboo screen and clung to the lantern, plunging the room into darkness. The young ninja slipped inside, used the evil monk's own sword to kill him and then slipped away, unseen. As the boy grew into a man, he called his growing knowledge *ninjutsu*, meaning the art of patience. The secrets of the shadow warriors were passed down through the generations, from father to son, ninja to ninja.

'He's not moving,' Hana whispered. Her gaze was fixed on the flat rock, where the shadow warrior's head was just visible.

'Perhaps he realizes we've seen him?' Tatsuya suggested. 'He knows there's no point trying to hide.'

I wondered how we could hope to defeat a warrior with the strength of ten men—one who was so confident that he saw no need to hide himself! I narrowed my eyes, sizing up the rock. Would the ninja leap on us from above, sword in hand? Or would he simply put a straw to his mouth and send a series of poison darts flying through the air?

We inched closer, and I saw the shadow take shape. His clothes were bumpy, almost a green colour. One more step and I laughed out loud. The shape behind the rock was no ninja. It was a bush, small and round, rooted into the rock!

'Kimi!' Tatsuya motioned for me to be quiet, but it only made me laugh harder.

Tatsuya shot me a furious look. 'This is no time for laughing, Kimi,' he whispered. 'You don't understand how ruthless ninja are!'

I grinned back at him. 'Well, if that's true, it will be the first time I have met a ruthless thorn bush.'

'A what?' Tatsuya stopped dead, hand on the hilt of his sword and an arrow still fitted to his bow. He frowned and peered ahead, then muttered a curse. 'It *is* a thorn bush.'

'Watch out,' I teased, nudging him with my elbow. 'Some of those thorn bushes have the skill of ten men, you know!'

Hana giggled. Angrily, Tatsuya disarmed his bow and rammed the arrow back into his sash. 'So

I made a mistake,' he muttered. 'Better to be cautious than dead.'

'You were never this jumpy back at the *dojo*,' I said.

'He never needed to be,' Hana said, suddenly serious. 'We've all got reason to be on our guard, Kimi. Uncle Hidehira wants us captured, and he wouldn't hesitate to send a whole army after us.'

Hana's words sobered me immediately. 'You're right,' I said, quickly scanning the horizon. 'We do need to be on our guard. Day and night. If we see anything suspicious, we tell each other.' I reached out and briefly touched Tatsuya's hand. 'I'm sorry,' I said. 'I didn't mean to make fun of you.'

Tatsuya nodded. 'I know,' he replied. 'And I'm sorry, too. I shouldn't be so jumpy.'

After we had passed the ninja bush, the pathway began to level out a little, taking us beneath pine trees and sturdy maples. The sun slid lower in the sky and light began to fade.

'Do you think we should try and find somewhere to sleep soon?' Hana asked.

Tatsuya nodded. 'I thought I saw a plume of smoke up ahead,' he said. 'If it's a village, then we might be able to find shelter there. We're far enough away from the *dojo* that the *jito* won't find us here.'

As twilight began to deepen, we came to a small meadow where we stopped for a moment to watch fireflies dancing, tiny pinpoints of light against the deep blue sky.

'Do you remember, Hana,' I murmured, 'how Mother used to say that she liked to believe fireflies were *kami* spirits?'

Hana nodded, her face sad. 'She said we should not weep for the dead because they were happy with the Buddha, and they showed us this by dancing across the sky.'

I felt the weight of Master Goku's ashes in the bundle on my sash. Soon he would be with the Buddha. We would take him to the temple at the foot of Mount Fuji, and our teacher would find eternal peace.

Tatsuya murmured a prayer for Master Goku and for Mister Choji. Hana and I joined in, our low voices drifting away through the trees. As we turned and left the meadow behind, I offered up to the heavens a silent prayer for my father and older brothers, too.

We walked on, and soon a light spring rain began to fall, soaking through our clothes. I was losing track of time. The pathway we were following became muddy, and our sandals slipped and slid. The hems of my long *hakama* trousers stuck to my ankles as the fabric absorbed the rain. Our kimonos, which had been so neat and white for Master Goku's funeral that morning, were streaked with dirt.

'I hope we find shelter soon,' Hana said, shivering.

As darkness settled around us, we came to the village Tatsuya had seen earlier. The path widened into a single packed-earth road where a group of wooden huts huddled together around a well. Thick smoke rose from holes in the steep thatched rooftops. I guessed that the rain must have driven everyone indoors, because the place seemed deserted.

One of the huts was slightly larger than the others, with a lean-to stable at the back. Flickering candlelight spilled out from behind a filthy bamboo screen, and there was a sudden burst of raucous laughter.

'That must be the village inn,' Tatsuya said, using his cuff to wipe rain from his face. 'Maybe we can go in for a little while and get dry.'

Hana hung back a little, looking doubtful. 'I've never been in a place like this before,' she said in a low, anxious voice.

'It'll be all right,' Tatsuya said to Hana. 'I won't let anything bad happen to you.'

Then Tatsuya pushed a heavy curtain aside and we stepped inside the inn to a small room lit by a couple of glowing lanterns. It was perhaps the size of six *tatami* mats. Some customers sat on cushions by the walls while a few thin, grey-haired old men were grouped around a smoking charcoal brazier. Beside it an enormous soup pot hung from an iron hook.

An innkeeper wearing a grubby apron tied over his kimono was pouring *sake* rice wine into a bowl for one of the old men. He glanced up as we entered, his round face splitting into a yellow-toothed grin.

'Welcome, welcome!' he said, his quick gaze darting over us, taking in our wet, travel-stained clothing and the swords at our waists. 'You look like weary travellers in need of food and warmth.' The innkeeper watched as we took off our shoes, and Hana wrung out her waist-length hair.

'We just want to rest for a moment, if you don't mind,' Tatsuya said.

'Hmm . . . ' said the innkeeper. 'Tell me, what are three youngsters like you doing travelling alone, and in such filthy weather?'

'We're taking a message from our father to his brother,' I said, as the innkeeper eyed me suspiciously. 'We won't be any trouble.'

'Fine, fine,' the innkeeper said, and wiped his hands on his grubby apron. 'Then you should come closer to the fire.' Some of the old men shuffled around to make room for us. 'First we'll get you warm and dry. And then you'll need some food in your bellies.' He flipped the lid off the soup pot and a lick of steam rose up, filling the air with the delicate scent of fish and fresh ginger. My stomach rumbled and I realized I was hungry. It had been a long time since we'd eaten our black bean and rice cakes by the hot springs that afternoon. 'And I'll find you a place to sleep.'

'We're sorry,' Hana said with a polite bow. 'But we have no money to pay you.'

'Don't you worry about that, child,' the innkeeper said airily, ladling soup and noodles into bowls. 'You can help me with some chores in the morning.' He winked at Hana and pressed a bowl into her hands. 'Here you go. Drink up!'

'You're very generous,' Hana said uncertainly, holding back her wide sleeve as she accepted the bowl.

The innkeeper patted her shoulder. 'My hospitality is famous in this part of the province. A hungry traveller is never turned away from my door, especially not one as pretty as you!'

Hana blushed. Still smiling, the innkeeper

turned to Tatsuya and me. 'Come on, you two boys. Come closer to the fire like your sister . . . '

Tatsuya and I knelt by the fire. We were so close to the brazier that our wet clothes began to steam as we sipped the soup. The old men began their gossiping again about life in the village.

When we had finished, the innkeeper gave us handfuls of deliciously sour pickled plums to chew. 'The inn is full, but like I said before—I've never yet turned away a customer. You can share a room in the stable out at the back.' He jerked his thumb over his shoulder.

'Thank you,' I said, bowing my head respectfully.

The innkeeper poured more *sake* for the old men and when he had shuffled away, the oldest-looking man leaned towards Tatsuya. 'I don't expect you've seen many other travellers on the road,' he said to Tatsuya. 'All the men have gone off to fight in the *jito*'s army.'

At the word '*jito*', one of the men who had been huddled in a dark corner nursing a bowl of *sake*, suddenly sat up. '*Jito* you call him, eh?' he muttered drunkenly. He had tangled black hair, which hung like ragged curtains either side of a thin, wolfish face. His brown kimono and *hakama* trousers were crumpled and even more travel-stained than our own. 'I tell you this—Yamamoto no Hidehira is no *jito*.' At the sound of Uncle's name, my heart fluttered wildly, beating against my ribs like a captured bird. I wanted to shout out my agreement, but I knew I could not draw attention to ourselves.

'Hidehira is an imposter,' the drunkard railed. 'A warlord who will tear this province apart!'

'Be quiet there,' the innkeeper said angrily. 'We'll have no talk of that sort in my inn.'

'We should talk while we still can!' the drunkard cried. 'Soon the *jito* will have us all clenched so tightly in his iron fist that we'll barely be able to breathe, let alone talk freely.'

As the ragged man carried on muttering, I gripped my soup bowl tightly and tried to concentrate on the last few flakes of fish that floated in the bottom.

'This province is changing,' the drunkard went on, his voice a little louder this time. 'They don't call Hidehira the *Kaminari* for nothing, you know. He will bring thunder down upon us . . .'

'Hush!' snapped the innkeeper.

But the drunkard ignored him and staggered to his feet. 'There is a great storm coming!'

'I think we've heard enough from you,'

muttered one of the old men. 'Why don't you be quiet, you drunken fool.'

'The greed of the Yamamoto lord will bring down the province,' he proclaimed, slurring slightly as he stared around the room with bright, feverish eyes.

Another of the old men cast an anxious look at the drunkard. 'Hush,' he whispered. 'The walls are thin, and spies are everywhere. If word gets back to the *jito*, we'll all be branded traitors . . .'

At that, the old men began to mutter among themselves. A few of them drew away as if to put distance between themselves and the drunkard. I guessed they didn't want to be associated with him. But it wasn't because they were loyal to Uncle Hidehira. They were afraid of him.

It made my heart ache to remember my father, and how hard he had worked to rule fairly and with justice. The people of the estates had respected him. Some had even loved him. But Uncle ruled through fear rather than respect.

The drunkard lurched unsteadily over to us. 'What d'you think?' he demanded, swaying slightly as he pointed a finger at me. 'You, boy! You think the same way as me, don't you?'

'I don't know what you mean,' I said, avoiding

his eye. 'We just wanted shelter for the night, and then to be on our way at daybreak.'

The drunkard swayed on his feet, staring down at me. Then, to my relief, he turned away. For a moment, I thought he was going to leave us alone, but then he dropped on one knee in front of Hana. 'A little girl,' he said in a low voice, gazing at her long black hair in wonder. 'I had a little girl once. She was so pretty and sweet . . . '

Agony etched across his face and for a moment I thought I saw his drunken eyes clear.

'What happened to your little girl?' asked Hana in an uncertain voice.

The drunkard closed his eyes as if he couldn't bear to look at Hana's face any more. 'She died,' he said tightly. He stood up and waved an imperious hand at the innkeeper. 'More *sake*!' he cried.

The innkeeper shook his head. 'You've had enough.'

'I've never had enough!' the drunkard exclaimed. 'Soon the fields of the province will be soaked with blood!'

But we didn't hear any more because the innkeeper had had enough. He marched over to the drunkard and hauled him up by the collar of his dirty kimono.

'You keep quiet,' he said, shaking the drunkard

so hard that his head snapped back. 'I don't know where you come from, but in these parts we speak kindly of the *jito* because he's the man in charge. Do you hear me?'

The drunkard stared blearily at the innkeeper. 'You're a fool . . . ' he slurred.

'Better a fool than an idiot soaked in *sake*,' the innkeeper said tightly. 'Now get out of my inn!' He bundled the drunkard to the door and tossed him out into the rain, kicking him in the backside. 'And don't show your ugly face round here again—you hear?'

I watched the innkeeper sweep the filthy curtain back across the doorway, shutting out the sight of the drunkard on his knees in the mud.

Hana and I exchanged a troubled glance. Things were desperate, even in this remote village. People were afraid of Uncle. They hid in their houses and inns, too scared even to speak his name.

The fields of the provinces will be soaked with blood, the drunkard had said.

Dread stole over me as I thought of the perilous future that lay ahead.

Chapter 8

Everyone soon settled down. The old
men sipped their *sake*, and the innkeeper
brought us tea. Tatsuya, Hana, and I
stayed by the fire until our clothes were dry, then
the innkeeper spotted us yawning.

'You'd better get to your beds,' he said with a
grin. 'You'll find sacks of hay to sleep on out in the
stables. Take this lantern. The stable's nice and dry,
and you should find plenty of blankets out there to
keep you warm.'

The leather pouch with Goku's ashes bounced
against my thigh as I stood up. Tatsuya took the
lantern and we said goodnight. Outside, the rain
was still falling and we had to make a dash for the

stable at the back of the inn, leaping around muddy puddles and laughing as we tried not to splash each other.

I pushed open the stable door and we stepped inside, stamping our feet and shaking the rain-water from our hair.

A low voice hissed out of the shadows at us. 'Keep the noise down, can't you? I'm trying to sleep!'

Swiftly Tatsuya swung the lantern round, and by its flickering light we could just make out the huddled shape of the drunkard who'd caused such a stir in the inn. He was sitting in one of the stalls with his back propped against the stable wall. A horse loomed over him, half-asleep, twitching its tail.

'Sorry,' Hana said, giving a little bow. 'We didn't know anyone else was in here.'

'Well, I'm in here,' the drunkard said flatly, his dark eyes flashing. 'And I'd appreciate it if you kept the noise down.'

Tatsuya and I nodded and began to tiptoe past him, but Hana lingered for a moment.

'The innkeeper was rough with you earlier,' she said, her voice soft with concern.

The drunkard shrugged. 'So what if he was?'

'Don't you have a home you could go to?' Hana persisted.

'I have many places I could go to,' the drunkard replied, staring up at her from between his curtains of ragged hair. 'But none are as warm and dry as this stable.'

I came back to stand beside Hana and stared down at the drunkard. The man returned my gaze with clear brown eyes. Beneath the grime, he looked young, his skin fresh and unlined.

'You don't seem as drunk now as you were earlier,' I observed.

He shrugged, an amused smile curving his lips. 'I may be drunk; I may not be,' he said. 'But either way, the innkeeper threw me out before I had to pay for my meal.' He paused and considered us. 'One thing is certain—I meant what I said about a storm coming. You youngsters would do well to deliver your message and then keep on walking. Leave this province and don't come back.' His eyes burned as he stared up at us. 'Those who stay within the *Kaminari*'s reach are doomed.'

Words like that, spoken above the hard drumming of rain on the stable roof, sounded like a prophecy. I had to stop myself shivering.

'Who *are* you?' Tatsuya asked, crouching down

beside the man. 'There is the look of the samurai about you. Yet you dress in rags and the scabbard of your sword is old and the metal decorations rusty.'

'You have a sharp eye, young man,' the man said with a wolfish grin. 'I was once a samurai—a captain for the old *jito*, Lord Yoshijiro. But I will never swear loyalty to his brother.'

Hana and I stared at him. This man had once been in Father's army, yet we had never been aware of him because of our position of privilege. I felt a moment of regret as I realized there must always have been people like this—anonymous, invisible, yet important for my family's safety and well-being.

'The code of the *bushi* says that you owe your loyalty to the *jito*,' Hana reminded him, her voice soft, 'whoever he may be.'

But the captain shook his head. 'I owe nothing to a lord who breaks the *bushi* code with every move he makes,' he muttered. 'Do you know Lord Hidehira is planning to invade estates in the Sagami province?' In disgust, he spat into the filthy straw that lined the floor of the stable, then wiped his mouth with the cuff of his kimono. 'Lord Yoshijiro spent years forging an alliance with Lord Kanahara of southern Sagami. And now his brother wants to smash the accord and go to war.'

I gazed at the captain, suddenly realizing that this was no ordinary drunk. Here was a man who had been close enough to my father to know about his political manoeuvres.

I crouched down beside Tatsuya, looking at the captain urgently. 'How do you know this?' I asked.

He glared back at me. 'I know because Lord Hidehira was recruiting troops to march east with his army. East to Sagami! I refused to join, so he had me stripped of all my possessions. Now I am *ronin*, a samurai with no master. And so I am forced to wander from place to place. This rusty sword was the best weapon I could get.'

We were all silent for a moment. Then the *ronin* captain glanced at each of us in turn. 'So what's your story?' he asked. 'You three have no loyalty to Lord Hidehira.'

I stared at him in surprise. Were we so obvious?

The captain grinned, looking even more wolfish than before. 'I thought as much,' he said with a nod. 'I wasn't certain, but your face has just told me the truth. You don't trust Hidehira any more than I do.' He clenched his fists. 'He will pay for what he did that night he murdered the true *jito* and his family. One day, I'll face his army on a battlefield and I'll have my revenge.'

His thoughts were so close to my own that it felt as though there was an invisible bond between us. A silken thread seemed to pull tight in the dry, stale air of the stable. It sounded as if he had even been there that horrible night.

'Were you there, then? At the *shinden* when it burned?' I whispered.

His eyes darkened, and Hana shuffled beside me. 'I was there. My daughter and wife did not survive.'

I took a deep breath. I could not go so far as to tell him the whole truth about Hana and me, but I trusted him enough to tell him that we were rebels. 'We are sworn to fight against Hidehira until death,' I admitted. 'We, too, lost loved ones that night.'

The captain grunted. 'If you want to fight against that rat then you should head east. Fight *with* Lord Kanahara's people against the *jito*.'

'Maybe we will head east,' Hana said gently. 'But we're not going anywhere tonight, and neither are you.' She lifted down a thick rough horse blanket and folded it around the captain's shoulders. 'It's late, and we all need to get some sleep.'

We said goodnight to the captain and moved

along to an empty stall at the back of the stable. I laid my leather pouch on a pile of soft straw. The lantern flickered and the rain drummed on the roof as we practised our *kata* and meditated, as Master Goku had taught us. Afterwards, we each took a horse blanket and made a row of beds.

Tatsuya blew out the lantern and we all settled down to sleep. I was too exhausted to even take down my hair. The others fell asleep quickly, their soft rhythmic breathing barely audible above the drumming rain. But I stayed awake for a while, pondering the captain's words, dreading a future under Uncle's rule. Could I stop him before he grew too powerful?

Master Goku would have known what to do—how to stop Uncle's plans. *Who will guide me now that my sensei is gone?* I wondered. After seeing Uncle dispatch the students in the temple, I knew I needed more skill, more strength, to have a hope of defeating him. Maybe in the morning, I could ask the *ronin* for a lesson.

At last I drifted into sleep, and dreamed of Mother and Moriyasu. They were standing hand in hand by one of the lily ponds at home. The sun was shining, and Moriyasu was smiling as he beckoned me to come and paddle with him in the warm water.

Then I heard whispering, and all at once the dream raced away. I was wide awake, eyes straining into the darkness, the smell of straw and horses strong in my nostrils. The rain had stopped. Was it the sudden silence that had woken me?

But then I heard whispering again, and my heart began to pound. There was someone else in the stable with us! Someone who crept across the hay-strewn floor as if they didn't want us to hear them coming.

No friend would move in such a way.

Realizing we had been too trusting, I shot my hand out to grab my sword. But in the next instant I realized it was gone. Thieves!

'Hana!' I threw off my blanket and scrambled up onto my knees. 'Tatsuya!'

But it was too late. At the sound of my voice, someone made a grab for me in the darkness. I struggled wildly, yelling as I tried to twist away. But powerful hands grasped my wrists and twisted them tightly behind my back. Pain lanced through my arms and into my shoulders.

Were these Uncle's men? Had someone overheard our dangerous conversation with the *ronin* captain?

Panic surged through me just as a deep voice growled close to my ear. 'Bring the light!'

All at once the door to the stable burst open and the innkeeper came rushing in. He held a lantern high and I blinked as bright light spilled into every corner of the stable.

I saw immediately that we were surrounded by three thin, weaselly-looking men. Their clothes were threadbare, and their greasy hair was tied in rough top-knots. One of them snatched up the leather pouch containing Master Goku's ashes and cradled it tightly to his chest. A greedy smile stretched across his face, as if he thought the pouch contained treasure. Horrified, I struggled hard.

'Stop that!' My captor twisted my wrists and a sharp pain shot up my arms.

Nearby, another man had Tatsuya in a head-lock, his wiry arms wrapped around poor Tatsuya's face and neck so he could barely breathe, much less struggle. But Hana was free! My heart leaped with hope as she made a desperate grab for her *nihonto* . . .

A third man pounced like a viper, kicking the sword away out of her reach. 'Not so fast,' he sneered, his teeth like yellow needles in the lantern light. Catching hold of Hana, he twisted her hands up behind her back and held her tightly, ignoring her desperate cries.

I looked around for the *ronin* captain. I prayed that he would help us—but his stall was empty. The only sign he had ever been there was a crumpled horse blanket in the corner. He must have moved on during the night, while we were sleeping.

'Let us go!' Hana cried, struggling to free herself.

The innkeeper ignored her. 'The boys aren't worth much,' he growled to his men. 'But this girl is so pretty. The slave trader will pay a good price for her.'

Sell Hana to a slave trader? No! I began to struggle violently. Tatsuya wrestled with his captor, trying to break free, but to no avail.

Meanwhile, Hana bucked and twisted, earning a cuff across the head from one of the men. 'Not her face,' barked the innkeeper. 'She won't be worth as much with bruises.'

'Their swords and this longbow must be worth something, too,' one of the men said, gathering up our weapons. He turned Moriyasu's bamboo *bokken* over in his big calloused hands and grinned. 'Even this toy may fetch a price.'

'Get your hands off that!' I yelled.

'Stop your squealing, pup,' snarled the

innkeeper. He gestured to his men. 'Gag them and tie their hands behind their backs.'

Immediately a filthy piece of rag was stuffed into my mouth. It tasted of dirt and sour milk. I tried to spit it out, but the man wrapped a second strip around my mouth and tied it tightly at the back of my head.

When we were all bound and gagged, the innkeeper grunted his satisfaction. 'We'll put them in the storeroom until morning,' he said. 'Then we'll take them to the coast and see what Mister Hoki says when he sees them.' He gripped Hana's chin in his hand, tilting her face up to the light. 'Mister Hoki is going to like the look of you, princess!'

Hana jerked her face away, struggling wildly.

They roughly dragged all three of us out of the stables and shoved us into a small storeroom off the kitchen at the back of the inn. We landed in a tangle of arms and legs as the screen door was snapped shut, and then we were alone in the darkness. I heard a clunk as a piece of wood was fitted across the screen to keep it closed.

I could see nothing in the inky darkness, but I could feel Hana on one side of me and Tatsuya on the other. We all struggled to free ourselves. The more we struggled the tighter our bindings seemed to get.

Abruptly I stopped struggling. Tatsuya and Hana stopped too, and for a long time we all just sat, breathing heavily through our noses, our mouths tightly gagged.

Think, Kimi. Think! I told myself. What would Master Goku do in this situation?

His voice washed through my mind like a hint of incense carried on a cool spring breeze. *A tranquil mind can often provide the answer to a warrior's dilemma* . . .

A tranquil mind? My mind certainly wasn't tranquil. It was in turmoil.

Deliberately, I tried to still my wild thoughts. I closed my eyes and let peace steal over me. My blood slowed. My breathing grew shallower. Time passed. And all at once, an answer came to me. If struggling made our bonds tighter, then perhaps careful, slow movements might ease them.

Slowly—so slowly—I felt my way around the loops that fastened my wrist. There were four of them in all. I tried each loop in turn until I found some slack. Fingers working, I fed the slack all the way around my wrist into the next loop, and then the next. The rope burned against the soft skin of my wrist. Then one of the loops eased. Just a little . . . but it was enough. I took a deep breath and pushed my wrists apart—and all at once my heart began to race with excitement.

My hands were almost free!

I prayed that whatever those men were doing to prepare their pack horses would take a few more moments. I shook my hand and the rope quickly uncoiled. I twisted my right hand free and reached for my gag . . .

Suddenly I became aware of a stealthy creaking sound on the other side of the storeroom. I heard the door jamb being lifted quietly and the screen door slid open. A shaft of light fell across me. I blinked, half blinded after being in the darkness for so long, and quickly hid my freed hands behind my back as the figure of a tall, powerful-looking man loomed in the doorway.

I couldn't make out his face, because the light was behind him. But my heart squeezed tight with fear when I saw the sharp steel blade of a *tanto* dagger glittering in his hand.

Chapter 9

Hana made a strangled sound through her gag, and Tatsuya struggled wildly.

But they were still tightly bound and I knew as the man strode forward into the room, that I would have to defend us by myself. I twisted my legs underneath me and desperately tried to push myself into a kneeling position.

Dropping onto one knee beside me, the man brought his *tanto* dagger slicing downwards in a sharp curve.

I whirled into an attack, slicing upwards, with one hand seizing the wrist of the hand that held the knife. My other hand pushed hard against his opposite shoulder, and as I hoped, the man's own body weight brought him down. Instantly I was up and on him, one knee pinning his dagger hand tightly to the floor.

I stared down into his face. By the glimmering light coming in through the open door, I found myself looking directly into the face of the *ronin* captain.

'You!' I exclaimed, after ripping off my gag.

My moment of shock was all he needed. He twisted out from under me and leaped away, dagger poised. I clutched the loops of rope still swinging from my left wrist. Could I use them as a weapon?

But then I noticed the captain was grinning.

'You have the heart of a brave warrior, my boy,' he said. He quickly re-sheathed his dagger and held his hands out, palms upwards, to show that he meant no harm. 'I was trying to cut you free,' he said. 'I thought you needed rescuing—but I was clearly wrong.'

I hurried over to Tatsuya and Hana. Together, the captain and I quickly untied them.

'I thought you'd gone,' I said, turning back to the captain. 'Moved on while we were sleeping.'

He shook his head. 'I slipped away when I heard the innkeeper and his friends outside. I thought they were coming for me . . . but when I heard them talking about the slave trader I decided to lie low and see if I could help you out.'

Her hands free, Hana tugged the filthy gag away from her mouth. 'Thank you,' she said.

The captain shrugged. 'We're allies, brothers in the fight against Lord Hidehira. And I can't afford to sacrifice a single brother!' He glanced out of the door and checked that no one was coming. 'Come on. Follow me! You have to get away from here before the innkeeper wakes up.'

'My sister and I aren't leaving without our swords,' I said firmly. 'And Tatsuya needs his longbow.'

The captain frowned. 'There's no time for that,' he said.

'There has to be,' I insisted. Not only did we want our weapons and Moriyasu's little *bokken*, but the thieves had taken Master Goku's ashes. I wasn't leaving without that pouch.

The storeroom led straight out into a small, filthy kitchen area lit by a single flickering lantern. There were two doors leading off the kitchen. I guessed that one must go through to the main room of the inn, where we had huddled by the fire. The other must be the door to the innkeeper's bed chamber. I pressed my ear to the thin wood-and-paper screen and listened.

For a moment I could hear nothing. Then I picked up the low-pitched rumbling sound of someone snoring.

I glanced at the others and put my finger to my lips. Slowly and quietly I slid back the screen door. The innkeeper was asleep on a mattress in the corner, flat on his back with his mouth wide open. He was still dressed in his grubby kimono. Fastened to his sash was a leather money bag about the size of my fist.

I scanned the room and spotted Master Goku's ashes. The pouch's string remained tightly knotted, and I prayed that it had not been tampered with. Heaped on the floor beside it were our swords, Moriyasu's *bokken*, and Tatsuya's longbow.

Tatsuya and Hana slipped past me and scooped up the weapons, holding them carefully so they wouldn't clink together. I stared in disgust at the snoring innkeeper. His tongue protruded from between his fleshy lips as he snored, and a film of greasy sweat covered his face.

My face flushed hot with rage as I remembered how kind he had seemed when we arrived, and yet all the time he must have been planning to sell us to a slave trader. I wondered how many other travellers he had betrayed in this way.

'Come on, Kimi,' Hana whispered, pressing my sword into my hand. 'Let's go.'

I shook my head. 'He should pay for his treachery,' I whispered fiercely.

'We've got what we came for,' Tatsuya whispered, slinging his longbow onto his shoulder. 'Now let's get out of here.'

I hesitated, weighing my sword in my hand. I couldn't just walk away from this betrayal.

Quietly, the captain came over, bent down, and carefully untied the leather money bag from the innkeeper's belt. 'You want him to pay?' he asked. 'Then take this.'

He pressed the money bag into my hand. It felt satisfyingly heavy, but was it enough for what he would have done to my sister? Was it enough for the others he must have sold into slavery?

'Come *on*, Kimi,' Hana whispered at the door.

At my sister's command, I sheathed my sword and backed away. Silently I slid the screen door closed behind me and together we crept out of the inn.

Outside, the clouds and rain had cleared. There was a half-moon high in the dark sky. Its bright light made the sleeping village look as if it was made entirely of blue and silver shadows.

The captain glanced around. 'You should go

now,' he told us. 'Deliver your message—and maybe one day our paths will cross again.'

'If we are both set against Lord Hidehira,' Hana said, 'I feel certain that they will.'

'Won't you come with us?' I asked, still sensing that there was much this wandering soldier could teach me.

He shook his head. 'My destiny lies elsewhere,' he said. 'But I am sure you and I will meet again.'

I opened the money bag, scooped out half the coins and pressed them into his calloused fingers. 'Thank you for saving us.'

We left him standing in a clearing in front of the stable, a tall, strong-looking figure silhouetted in a patch of silver moonlight. I waved, and the captain raised one hand in a silent farewell. Then I turned and walked away with Hana and Tatsuya.

The final part of our journey to Mount Fuji had begun.

Before long we had left the sleeping village far behind and soon the peak of the mountain loomed ahead of us, rising up from the dark landscape. We struck out along the pathway towards it, carefully picking our way in the moonlight. Hana had agreed to put her hair back into a boyish topknot, so that no one would realize that she was a girl. The incident with the innkeeper had shown us that girls could attract the wrong sort of attention. We would be safer if passers-by thought we were boys.

'We must keep alert for anyone following us,' Tatsuya said, as we walked.

I focused my mind, stretching my senses for any sound or change in the air. But we didn't see or hear anyone else. I wondered whether the innkeeper had woken yet. Had he discovered our disappearance?

A small measure of satisfaction curled through my belly as I imagined his rage upon finding the storeroom empty, but somehow that was not enough. We had the leather money bag, certainly, but I wished there had been some other revenge. I should have emptied out all his jugs of *sake*. Or perhaps cut a *kanji* into his cheek with the point of my sword, so that everyone who looked at his face would know him for a liar and a cheat!

I clenched my fists tightly.

Tatsuya was walking behind me. 'You're thinking about the innkeeper, aren't you?' he said.

'It makes me angry that he boasted about never turning a traveller away from his inn,' I muttered. 'How many others have woken up to find themselves prisoners? We should have tied him up in a sack and left him somewhere in the forest. That would have frightened him!'

Hana was leading the way, and she glanced back over her shoulder at me. 'I understand why you want revenge, Kimi,' she said quietly. 'But Father would have said that revenge eats away at the soul. Eventually it destroys the person who seeks it.'

I felt the heavy pouch on my sash, and shivered as night closed in around us. Somewhere an owl hooted. The moon was high over my shoulder, casting my shadow ahead of me on the stony path and for a while it seemed as though my own shadow was leading me onwards.

At last the red glow of sunrise streaked the sky to the east. Creatures began to stir in the undergrowth either side of the path and I heard the rasping croak of a frog somewhere far away.

'It will be light soon,' Hana said.

The morning air was sharp and clean after the rain of the previous evening. As light flooded the landscape, I saw Mount Fuji ahead. My spirits soared as I thought of Mother and Moriyasu.

'We're making good progress,' I said as we forged ahead.

Late that afternoon, our narrow path widened and joined with another path which cut through a pine forest.

Suddenly a group of chattering peasant women rounded the corner ahead, and there was no time for us to get off the road.

'Keep walking,' I murmured to the others.

We kept our heads down and hurried past. The women ignored us, as if seeing strangers on the road was nothing unusual. Soon a team of pack horses lumbered past, their hooves churning up the mud as it headed north. It was followed by a man in a brown kimono driving an ox cart. Three ragged children danced along behind him, all of them carrying baskets and bundles.

'We must be approaching a village or town,' I said to Hana.

Moments later we came over the crest of a small hill and saw a little town nestled in a fold of hills at the foot of Mount Fuji.

'Oh, look!' Hana cried. 'We're almost there.'

I shaded my eyes, studying the wooden huts that huddled together inside the town's walls. A single main street cut through the town, leading up a gentle hill towards a cluster of grey rooftops lit by the warm sunshine of late afternoon.

'Is that the temple?' I asked Tatsuya, pointing.

He narrowed his eyes for a moment, squinting against the sun. 'I think so,' he said.

'Our meeting place with Mother,' I said, my heart beginning to flutter with joy.

'Perhaps she's already there—waiting for us,' Hana said.

I smiled, imagining Mother standing serenely with Moriyasu's little hand clasped tightly in hers.

'Come on,' I said, grabbing Hana's hand.

We hurried along the pathway and joined the crowds of farm workers and peasants making their way to the town. One or two of them had shaven heads and wore yellow monks' robes. I wondered if they were heading to the temple as we were. I became conscious of the weight of the ashes on my sash. I hoped that when we reached the temple, there would be a priest who would accept Master Goku's remains.

The road grew busier as we neared the town. All around us, people chattered loudly, some of them jostling each other good-naturedly. Hope buzzed through my limbs, and Hana was smiling all the time as she looked around her. But I soon noticed that Tatsuya seemed ill at ease. He kept glancing back over his shoulder as though he thought someone was following us.

I fell into step beside him. 'I don't see anyone suspicious,' I told him.

'I don't either,' Tatsuya admitted. 'But I don't have to see them. I can *feel* them. There's definitely someone watching us.'

His words made me shiver. 'Have you had this feeling before?' I asked quietly.

'Once,' he replied. He glanced over his shoulder and then looked directly at me, his eyes dark pools of fear. 'The night my father disappeared.'

At the *dojo*, Tatsuya had told us about one moonlit night long ago, when he had followed his father to the village shrine, only for his father to disappear at the hands of a man in black. Tatsuya never saw his father again.

'Do you think the men who took your father were ninja?' I asked hesitantly.

Tatsuya bit his lip. 'I don't think it,' he said. 'I *know* it.'

My heart skipped a beat. 'Are they here? Now?'

Tatsuya opened his mouth, but before he could respond, Hana suddenly grabbed my wrist. 'Not ninja,' she whispered urgently. 'Soldiers!'

I saw two samurai in full armour standing either side of the gateway to the town. The late afternoon sun burnished their iron helmets to a dull reddish-gold and the spears cast long black shadows across the road. Their eyes seemed to bore into the face of everyone who passed.

'They're looking for us,' Hana said flatly. She pulled me back so that we were walking behind a pack horse burdened with baskets.

Keeping pace with the horse, I peered past the baskets and studied the two samurai carefully. Neither of them seemed to be wearing the distinctive red silk *mon* badge that would mark them as Uncle's men. 'I don't think so, Hana,' I murmured. 'They're just the town guards.'

'Uncle Hidehira's men will have got here before us,' Hana insisted. 'They will have told the town guard to look for us, and block our entry.'

'It might be a good idea to split up,' Tatsuya said quietly, slowing his pace and dropping back. 'If they are looking for us, they'll expect to see three youngsters walking together. I'll catch you up again when we're safely past.'

Hana and I kept our heads down, and the horse between us and the two samurai. Keeping pace with the crowd, we walked beneath the high curving wooden gateway and entered the town. With a sigh of relief, I realized the samurai were behind us.

Inside the town, there were no other guards in sight. The busy main street led uphill towards the temple, criss-crossed by a warren of narrow alley-ways. I stared around me, drinking in the experience of being in a busy town. The street was chaos, but a happy chaos that lifted my spirits. There were shops and stalls and women bending over looms at the side of the road, their fingers busily weaving silk. Bamboo bird cages swung from poles. Shelves bowed under the weight of porcelain bowls and cups, and barrels of *sake* wine. Chatter bubbled up like music in the warm spring air.

I exchanged a secret, amused look with Hana. Many years ago, as a family, we had made the long journey to the Imperial Capital, but remained hidden inside a curtained palanquin. We had never walked on foot before in a place as busy as this, as the sound of the crowd swelled the air around us.

Safely inside the town, Tatsuya quickly caught up with Hana and me. Together we pushed our way through the crowd, heading along the main street in the direction of the temple.

I caught a whiff of something delicious—a hot savoury smell that reminded me we hadn't eaten since the previous night.

Beside me, Hana's mouth was open and I knew she was feeling the hunger. Tatsuya saw, too, and put a gentle hand under her elbow. 'Food,' he said in a firm voice. 'We must stop for a moment and get something to eat.'

A nearby stall was selling pieces of sizzling chicken stuck onto bamboo skewers. '*Yakitori* chicken!' bawled the stall-holder, his cheerful face red from bending over a blazing charcoal brazier.

I remembered that I had the innkeeper's money bag tucked into my sash, and pulled it out. But what should I do? I'd never bought anything before. The servants had always done it for me . . .

Tatsuya saw my hesitation. 'I can help, Kimi.'

While Tatsuya negotiated with the *yakitori* seller, I looked at the stalls on either side of his. Both were piled high with dishes of food—sticky rice balls, sour plums, strips of smoked fish.

I was surprised to see so many provisions, because the towns and villages around the *dojo* had been bled dry. Food was scarce and many people were starving. I guessed that it was just a matter of time before Uncle Hidehira's draining grip reached this far from his seat of power.

Coins clinked into the seller's chubby fist, and Tatsuya handed Hana and me portions of *yakitori* chicken. We ate them immediately, tearing the meat from the skewers with our teeth as we walked. Hot grease dripped down my fingers and stained my cuffs, but I didn't care. Nothing mattered now—we were almost at the end of our journey, so close to seeing Mother again. As long as we all managed to evade Uncle's evil grasp, our family would be reunited.

I wiped my hands on the hem of my jacket, and glanced ahead. Further along the street I could see the temple tower clearly, silhouetted against the sinking sun. We were so nearly there.

'We must hurry,' I whispered. 'There's not much time.'

Moving quickly, we weaved through the crowd. Ahead of us a thick knot of people jostled and bunched up, then broke apart as someone rapped out a sharp order. A spear danced above the heads of the townspeople, sparkling as it caught the sunlight. A samurai appeared, followed by another and another. They shouldered their way through the throng, sharp eyes scanning left and right.

My heart stopped beating for a moment as I caught sight of a red silk *mon* badge fluttering in the breeze. Uncle's men!

Hana clutched my wrist and I knew she had spotted them, too. We glanced at each other in horror. The crowd seemed to close in on either side of us. The sun was sinking fast, a shimmering ball of red fire. As it dipped behind the grey tile rooftops, the shadows around us deepened.

A moment ago the busy street had seemed a place of safety and hope. Now it felt dangerous.

Tatsuya was frowning and his hand rested lightly on the scabbard of his sword. 'Don't make any sudden moves,' he murmured. 'We mustn't do anything to draw attention to ourselves.'

Hana nodded. 'We're just country boys visiting the town,' she said softly, as the samurai pushed their way along the street, coming closer with every step. 'Just taking in the sights and buying a few bits and pieces before closing time. There are dozens of others just like us. The samurai won't be able to tell us apart from the real farm workers.'

The soldiers were so close now that I could hear the thumping of their leather boots. Quickly I turned aside and began to inspect the eels and herring laid out on a fish-seller's table. Tatsuya and Hana drifted casually to the next stall and pretended to be interested in a pile of wide straw hats. As the soldiers passed, Hana lifted down one of the hats and held it up to hide her face, turning it in her hands like an enormous golden wheel.

One of the soldiers passed so close to me that I could smell the lacquer he'd used to harden his leather armour. Blood pounded in my ears as I waited for a shout of recognition. But he didn't even slacken his step. He marched on with the others and the crowd closed behind them.

I felt weak with relief.

But almost immediately I spotted another samurai further on, and then another. It looked as if there was one stationed on every corner! Red silk *mon* badges seemed to line the street all the way to the wooden temple gate at the far end.

Tatsuya pulled a face. 'We're going to have to be clever if we don't want to be seen.'

'We could go down one of these side alleys,' Hana suggested. 'Perhaps take another route to the temple?'

I glanced down the nearest alley. The walls seemed to close in, making the narrow space seem dark and dangerous. I shook my head. 'Too easy to get trapped.'

Hana took a deep breath. 'Then we should be on our guard.'

We kept walking and I tried to look casual, but inside my stomach was a tight knot of fire. I forced myself not to look at the samurai as we passed them, but instead to be interested in the market stalls. What fascinating lanterns! What intricately painted scrolls!

Gradually, we neared the end of the main street. I could see the temple entrance not far away. Two enormous carved *nio* guardian statues stood on either side, the wood painted blue, green, and gold. We were nearly there . . .

I became aware of a pair of eyes boring into me and glanced up to meet the gaze of a fierce-looking samurai. Did he recognize me? I couldn't tell. His helmet was pulled down low so that his face was almost entirely in shade, but his eyes gleamed like chips of black flint. He frowned and took a step towards me, and then another.

'I think I've been spotted,' I whispered desperately to Tatsuya and Hana.

'Keep walking,' Tatsuya said firmly.

'But—'

'Just keep walking. I'll deal with this.' Tatsuya dropped back and suddenly melted into the crowd.

The samurai took another step towards me, and shouted to me, 'You! Come here!'

My heart began to hammer against my ribs. I glanced hurriedly around, looking for a place to hide. There was only a stall selling beautiful silk sashes in rainbow colours. Perhaps I could duck behind the table, and . . .

Suddenly a shout tore the air, and I recognized

Tatsuya's voice raised in alarm. 'Thief!' he bellowed. 'That samurai is a thief!'

People turned to look. I caught a glimpse of Tatsuya. He made a frantic gesture to me which seemed to say, *Disappear now!* and then bellowed again, 'The samurai is a thief!'

'What are you talking about?' the samurai turned and glared at Tatsuya. 'I'm no thief.'

'If you're no thief,' an old woman said loudly, 'then what's that sticking out of your armour?'

The samurai whipped round, patting himself down. All at once his hand brushed against a bright green strip of silk that had been tucked between two plates of armour.

'That's one of my sashes!' cried a nearby stallholder.

The crowd pushed forward and surrounded the samurai.

'What a disgrace!' muttered a woman in a rich silk kimono, fluttering her fan in front of her face.

'He brings dishonour to the name of samurai,' sneered a burly, black-haired man with two swords at his waist. He caught hold of the soldier's arm. 'I think you'd better give that back . . . ' he began menacingly.

I didn't hear the rest. Hana caught my hand and together we fled up the street.

chapter 6

Behind us, pandemonium broke out. I could hear the samurai protesting his innocence, and the stall-holder crying, 'I want him arrested!'

At last the sounds faded, just as Tatsuya caught up with us.

'That was so clever,' I said.

Hana gave Tatsuya a hug. I noticed a blush creep up Tatsuya's cheeks as he raised his eyebrows in surprise.

'Come on,' I said. 'We're nearly at the temple. I doubt if the monks will allow soldiers to patrol on sacred ground, so we should be safe in there.'

Inside the temple grounds, a stone path led up a gentle slope lined with cedar trees. As we walked, a feeling of peace and calm settled on me. The pathway was smooth beneath my feet, and I could hear the distant music of trickling water. I thought how perfect this place would be as a final resting place for Master Goku.

We passed a few people walking in the opposite direction, leaving the temple. Then at the end of the path we came to a courtyard edged with green ferns. In the centre, a small waterfall tumbled over a stream. A pilgrim in yellow robes and a peasant woman were both scooping water from the waterfall into bowls to wash their hands and purify themselves before they approached the main temple buildings.

Tatsuya, Hana, and I stopped at the fountain. We let the clear, cool water play over our fingers for a moment. I looked around alertly, centring myself in my surroundings. Was Mother here? Would she see us and come hurrying over, or would we need to seek her out? I glanced at each of the temple buildings in turn, wondering where we should start our search.

The hall, or *honden*, the study hall, and two-storey main gate building were clustered in a horseshoe shape around the edges of the courtyard, their intricately carved rooftops streaked orange by the last of the late-afternoon sunlight. A few people were just leaving the *honden* hall. A chubby priest in sandals and long crimson robes bowed to them as they walked beneath a string of bright blue and yellow prayer flags. He had a broad, cheerful face.

I turned to Hana. 'We should speak to him about Master Goku,' I said in a low voice. Quickly I pulled the pouch from my sash and, with Hana and Tatsuya beside me, I crossed the courtyard towards him.

The priest turned to watch us approach. Then, as his good-natured gaze took in Hana's boyish clothes but delicate features, a wary expression passed over his face. He glanced at me, and then at the pouch in my hand—and turned as pale as ash.

He came hurrying towards us and took my arm, steering me gently in the direction of a small building just visible behind the *honden* hall. My breath caught in my throat. Did the priest know us? Was he loyal to Uncle Hidehira? I gripped the pouch in one hand and began to reach down for my sword with the other . . .

But the priest's next words reassured me. 'You run a great risk in coming here,' he whispered,

129

checking over his shoulder to see that no one had followed us.

'Do you know who we are?' Hana asked in astonishment.

The round-faced priest ushered us quickly inside the small building. Shadows fell around us. The air was scented with jasmine.

'I should think every man, woman, and child between here and the northern provinces knows who you are,' he said. 'The town has been swarming with samurai since dawn. We've had horsemen at the gates demanding to be let in. Of course we turned them away. This is a sacred place, a holy place. We do not allow soldiers here.' He turned to me. 'They are looking for fugitives who they say are thieves. Two girls. A woman. A young boy. They are to be captured and taken to the *jito*, where justice will be dispensed.' He narrowed his eyes. 'But I know the *jito*, and I know there will be no justice.'

'You know Hidehira?' I asked.

The priest gave a quick nod. 'I knew him and his brother well,' he said. 'A long time ago . . . another life . . . '

I gazed at him, scarcely able to take in what he said. This priest had known my father?

He looked at me for a moment and then at

Hana. 'I knew them both well enough to know that you are Yoshijiro's daughters,' he said at last.

For a moment I could barely breathe. The walls of the tiny building seemed to close in on me. Hana and I had held our secret close for so long that it seemed incredible that someone could simply look at us and know who we were.

The priest put a reassuring hand on my shoulder. 'You are safe here,' he said quietly. 'All three of you. I can only guess what you have been through these past moons—but I know enough about Master Goku's death and the desecration of his funeral to know that your spirit has suffered a torment.'

'You've heard about the funeral?' I asked. 'News travels quickly.'

The priest nodded. 'News always travels quickly,' he said. 'But it carries even faster when you have a network of rebels strung out across the countryside, like beads.'

'A rebel network,' Hana said, sounding breathless. 'Then you will know even better than we do what is happening at the *dojo*.'

'Indeed,' the priest said. 'In the absence of any other master, your uncle has put one of his generals in charge of the school. Many students have left in disgust. Most of them have returned to their families, but a few have joined a local rebel group.'

I exchanged a quick glance with Hana and Tatsuya and knew that they were wondering, as I was, whether Ko and Sato were among them.

'And now you have come here seeking sanctuary,' the priest continued. 'I cannot let you stay here—it would be too dangerous for you. There are only a dozen of us here, monks and priests. We are trained as warriors, yes. But we could not protect you if Hidehira's troops decided to storm the temple.'

'We don't expect you to protect us,' I said quickly. 'We aren't looking for shelter. We are to meet someone here at sundown and then move on.'

The priest looked again at the pouch in my hand. 'And this?' he asked with a curious expression on his face.

I bit my lip. 'This pouch contains the mortal remains of Master Goku.'

The priest gasped and for a moment I thought he would fall to his knees. He reached out a trembling hand and lightly touched the top of the bundle. 'The great Master Goku,' he whispered. 'He was my teacher once. And you have brought him here to Mount Fuji, where he was born?'

I nodded, and quickly explained how once Uncle Hidehira had declared he would scatter Goku's bones beneath the hooves of his conquering army, I couldn't leave him there.

'Will you keep his ashes here?' Hana asked, as I fell silent.

'Of course I will,' the priest said, bowing deeply. 'I will oversee the ritual myself.'

I held out the pouch. The priest took it reverently and placed it beside a small altar nearby, where a ribbon of incense drifted up into the still air. 'Master Goku's spirit will rest easily now that he has come home,' he said quietly, taking a pinch of incense and holding it first to his chest, then to his forehead before he dropped it into the burner. He began to chant, his voice soothing and harmonious.

I stood for a moment, mesmerized, my mind awash with memories of Master Goku.

Hana touched my arm. 'It is time to go to the *honden*,' she whispered.

The priest stopped chanting and turned to bow. 'The Buddha will go with you,' he said, blessing us.

I felt a weight lifted from me; we had delivered Goku to his final sanctuary and now we could complete our own journey.

We hurried out of the small building and made our way quickly across the courtyard to the *honden*. The last rays of the dying sun filtered through the cedar trees as we entered the great hall.

There were several worshippers in the dimly-lit interior. Some were kneeling to pray, the air around them wreathed with blue ribbons of incense. Others were putting up *ema*, the little wooden plates on which they had written their hopes and dreams.

I looked at each and every face inside the *honden*. There were several women dressed in dark kimonos, faces pale and serene. But none of them were my mother.

'We'll wait for her,' Hana said.

'It will look suspicious if we just stand here,' Tatsuya said cautiously, glancing around. 'Let's go and light some incense.'

He moved slowly away from us and went to kneel by the nearest altar. Beside me, Hana folded her hands and gazed around at the ornate statues and carvings of the Buddha. She seemed lost in thought. Her face had taken on a look of dreamy contemplation, a kind of serenity that I had not seen since before the death of Master Goku.

'Mother has been here,' she said at last, her voice soft. 'I can feel her presence.'

A tingle went up my spine. I gazed around, trying to visualize Mother's graceful form moving among the monks in their robes, the worshippers, the statues. Was she still here? Had she perhaps moved into a different, smaller hall of the *honden* to offer up a prayer for Father and my brothers?

I glanced back at the entrance and saw that the sun had slipped low in the sky. Long shadows lay across the clearing outside. It was almost closing time, and already a few of the monks were gently ushering worshippers towards the door.

Hana and I approached the altar where Tatsuya was kneeling on a small flat cushion. We settled down with him to wait for Mother to come. I wished suddenly that I had been able to read her last letter for myself. Perhaps there had been other instructions? I didn't know how long we should wait. Or even whether Mother would approach us, or if she wanted us to go to her.

Frowning thoughtfully, I took a pinch of incense and added it to the burner. A spiral of fragrant smoke twisted up into the air. Behind us, bare feet whispered on the polished wooden floor as the temple slowly emptied.

We waited. And we waited. But still Mother did not come.

'Perhaps we should go to look for her?' I whispered to Hana.

But my sister shook her head. 'Mother will find us when the time comes,' she whispered back.

A monk approached us. The hem of his saffron-yellow robe rippled around his ankles as he bowed politely. 'My apologies,' he whispered. 'I do not wish to disturb your prayers, but the temple is now closing.'

'Thank you,' Tatsuya said, bowing his head respectfully in return. 'Would it be possible for us to have a little more time? We are waiting for someone. We have arranged to meet them here in the *honden* at sundown, you see.'

The monk smiled kindly. 'A few more moments then,' he said, and moved away.

Silence settled around the three of us again. The temple was so quiet it was almost eerie. Somewhere a deep gong sounded, just once, the sound echoing through the building. There was a loneliness to the sound that made me feel cold inside.

Hana looked at me in dismay. 'A single strike of the gong signals closing time, Kimi.'

Just then a sudden movement at the side of the temple caught my eye. I glanced up to see a figure moving in the shadows, and my heart fluttered. Someone was coming out of one of the other halls. It had to be Mother!

I would have leaped to my feet and run across the temple towards her—but Hana put a gentle hand on my arm.

'It's not Mother,' she said, her voice so quiet that I could barely hear her.

'What—?' Confused, I stared at the front of the temple.

Just then the figure stepped forward out of the shadows. Flickering candlelight revealed a young man, wiry and strong, wearing *hakama* trousers and a short dark kimono jacket. A dagger and a long curved sword were fastened at his waist. One sleeve of his kimono was pinned tightly, where he had lost an arm.

'It's Manabu!' I whispered to Hana in amazement.

'Who is Manabu?' Tatsuya asked with a frown, as he watched Manabu come towards us. The servant was glancing around apprehensively as if to make sure he wasn't being followed.

'He is—*was*—one of Father's trusted servants,' I said, scrambling to my feet in excitement. 'Mother must have sent him to meet us!'

Tatsuya put up a hand to hold me back, but I

shrugged him off and ran headlong across the temple.

'Manabu!' I cried.

The servant looked at me in confusion. 'What do you want, boy?' he asked gruffly, and I realized that he did not know Hana and I had been disguised as boys.

'It's me—Kimi,' I said.

Manabu's eyes widened. He glanced around as if to check that no one else was nearby. 'Hush, Kimi-*gozen*, do not speak so loudly,' he begged, taking me by the elbow and guiding me into a shadowy alcove where we were half-concealed by an enormous bronze statue of the Buddha. 'There are spies everywhere.'

'I'm sorry,' I said with a bow. 'I am just relieved to see a friendly face.'

Hana and Tatsuya came to join us, and Manabu studied us all cautiously. His gaze lingered on Tatsuya's face. 'Who are you?' he asked with a frown.

'This is our friend, Tatsuya,' Hana told Manabu, drawing Tatsuya forward with a hand on his sleeve. 'Tatsuya was a student at the *dojo* with us, and has helped us on our journey.'

Tatsuya gave a short bow.

Manabu bowed stiffly in return. 'Pleased to

make your acquaintance, young master.' But as he turned to me, he looked anxious. 'Can this Tatsuya be trusted?' he whispered.

Tatsuya heard him, and bristled instantly. 'Surely the question should be—can *you* be trusted?' he shot back.

For a moment, they stared at each other. Tatsuya's eyes were narrow and full of suspicion.

At last Manabu shrugged and dropped his gaze. Turning back to me, he reached his only hand into the folds of his clothes and pulled out a paper scroll, rolled and wrapped with a crimson ribbon.

My heart beat faster. 'That's one of Mother's letters,' I said breathlessly. 'Is she here, Manabu?'

Chapter 11

Manabu took a breath, and I held mine. All my hopes were centred on seeing Mother's face, holding her hands, and hearing her tell me that everything was going to be all right.

Ever since the moment when Uncle Hidehira had read Mother's letter, I had believed that I would see her here today, at sundown. And now at last Hana and I were at the end of our journey. Mother was here—somewhere.

I couldn't resist glancing once more at the entrance to the other halls of the temple.

'The mistress is safe and well,' Manabu said. 'She asked me to come here and meet you in her place.'

I stared at Manabu in astonishment, crushed by the huge weight of disappointment. In an instant, my hopes had been blown away, like cherry blossom petals in a sudden gust of wind. For a moment I couldn't speak. It felt as if I was never meant to find her.

'But I don't understand,' Hana said to Manabu, her face anxious. 'I felt Mother's presence here in the *honden*. She was here . . . I'm sure she was!'

Tatsuya touched her hand comfortingly.

'You're right, Hana-*gozen*,' Manabu said, bowing his head slightly. 'Your mother has been here, many times. This temple has become her regular place of worship during our stay on the outskirts of town. She would have been here today. But when we saw a troop of the *jito*'s samurai come galloping in through the town gates this morning, we became afraid. The mistress could not risk herself or young Moriyasu-*gozen* being captured. She decided it would be safer for her to slip away to a new hiding place, while I came here to deliver this letter. The soldiers would not be looking for me.'

He held out the scroll letter to me. I saw immediately that it had been written on the same paper as my mother's other letters. My hands trembled as I took it from Manabu.

'The letter explains everything, Kimi-*gozen*,' Manabu said. 'You must read it, and then I will take you to her.' His good hand went to rest on the hilt of his sword. 'I am to keep watch for soldiers and protect you on your journey.'

I was about to untie the scroll when Manabu glanced again at Tatsuya. With a look of warning, he took my elbow and steered me a few steps away. 'Kimi-*gozen*, I don't want to intrude, but should you read the letter in front of this . . . this boy?' he said in a low, tight voice. 'What do you actually know about him?'

I hesitated, turning the scroll in my hands. 'He's a friend, Manabu,' I said. 'He's protected Hana and me during our journey here. I would trust him with my life.'

Manabu didn't look convinced, but he gave a quick nod. 'All right,' he said. 'I will trust him if you say I should . . . '

'I do,' I said firmly.

I turned back to see that Hana and Tatsuya were standing together.

'I just don't like him . . . ' Tatsuya was saying.

'You're just jumpy because of the innkeeper,' Hana said in a low, coaxing voice. 'But some people *can* be trusted, Tatsuya.' She beckoned Manabu over to stand beside her. 'Manabu was one of our father's trusted servants. Kimi and I always imagined that he had died the night of the massacre. But—' she turned to Manabu, 'we are so grateful that you helped Mother and Moriyasu to escape.'

Tatsuya softened but asked, 'Well, why doesn't he just tell us where your mother is and we can go straight to her?'

Manabu looked uncomfortable. 'My apologies, young master,' he said apologetically. 'I cannot tell you where the mistress is, because I do not know. She was worried that I might be captured and forced to tell where she was hiding, so she thought it would be safer if she wrote the code down in the letter that Kimi-*gozen* is holding in her hands. She said it would be something only her daughters could understand.'

'Open it, Kimi,' Hana urged.

I tugged the ribbon free and was about to unfurl the scroll when a gentle cough interrupted us.

I glanced up to see the young monk in yellow robes.

'The temple is closing,' he said with an apologetic smile. 'I must request that you all leave now.'

'Of course.' I quickly tucked the scroll into my

wide sleeve and gave a polite bow. 'Thank you for your patience and kindness.'

Hana and I made our way towards the doorway with Manabu. I glanced over my shoulder to see that Tatsuya was coming along behind us, his face closed and thoughtful.

Outside in the temple clearing, the first stars of the evening were dotted high above the cedars.

Just outside the gate, Manabu glanced around anxiously. 'We must be careful, Kimi-*gozen*,' he muttered, guiding us into a hiding place among the green ferns and cedar trees. 'It's not safe to linger out in the open.'

A light breeze rustled through the branches of the trees around us as I pulled off the ribbon and carefully unfurled the scroll. It wasn't pitch dark yet, so there was just enough light left to read Mother's elegant brush-strokes and perfect *kanji*. Hana came to stand close beside me. She let out a long, slow breath.

As I stared down at the scroll, everything seemed to blur. A single tear dropped onto the paper, making the ink blossom and spread. I bit my lip and carefully blotted the wet ink with my thumb.

I read the letter aloud to the others, my heart fluttering.

My dearest daughters,

I wanted so much to be at the temple today to meet you in person and behold your sweet faces once again. But alas our meeting has become impossible. A troop of samurai soldiers arrived in the town this morning. They are questioning people about two fugitives, and it is my belief that your uncle is searching for Moriyasu and me.

In order to keep your little brother safe, I must hide in a place where only you girls can find me.

Seek, and you will find us in the place of Hana's favourite poems.

Hana's favourite poems?

The blood in my veins leaped with excitement because I knew what Mother meant! I turned to Hana.

'*Fujigoko* . . . ' she said breathlessly, meeting my gaze with wide, excited eyes. 'The five lakes that ring Mount Fuji to the north. We saw one of them on our journey here.'

I nodded eagerly, clasping her hand. 'There are six poems about Fujigoko,' I said, 'each one detailing the beauty of the water at each lake, and the majesty of the mountain.'

But which of the five lakes had Mother and Moriyasu chosen as a hiding place?

'The lakes cover a wide area,' Manabu said with an anxious frown. 'Isn't the mistress more specific than that?'

I consulted the letter again, re-reading Mother's words. Her *kanji* had been dashed off quickly, her haste betrayed by the quick upward sweep of the brush-strokes and a rogue blot of ink at the edge of the scroll.

'No,' I said, shaking my head. 'There's nothing more . . . '

'Wait!' Hana interrupted, putting out her hand and tilting the top of the scroll. 'There's something written on the back. It's so small that we wouldn't have seen it when the paper was rolled up.'

Manabu leaned closer. 'What does it say, Kimi-*gozen*?'

I read aloud.

You know that the sixth poem contains

all five elements—Wood, Fire, Earth,

Metal, Water.

Oh, my dearest daughters. Nothing can

break the strength of all five elements

when they are together.

'What can the mistress mean by that?' Manabu asked.

'I'm not sure,' Hana said thoughtfully. She leaned against my arm to look at the scroll. 'The sixth poem was always my favourite . . . I used to love hearing Mother read it to me, because it talked about the most easterly of all the lakes, Yamanaka, and told of the swans that nested there.'

'I remember that,' I said with a nod. 'So she and Moriyasu must have chosen that lake as their hiding place.'

I rolled up the paper scroll and tucked it into my kimono. 'How far is it to Fujigoko?' I asked Tatsuya.

He thought for a moment. 'Less than a day's walk from here,' he said.

'So if we travel under cover of night, we could be with Mother and Moriyasu by tomorrow morning,' Hana said.

Tatsuya nodded. 'We'll make it easily if we set out now.'

I glanced at Manabu, who was looking concerned. 'Kimi-*gozen*,' he said hesitantly. 'There are soldiers everywhere. Don't you think it would be easier to hide if there were just three of us? Four is too many . . . ' He shot a meaningful glance at Tatsuya.

Why didn't Manabu trust him? Tatsuya was our friend. I would trust him with my life! I shook my head. 'We stay together,' I said firmly.

We left the temple grounds by the main gate. The pathway was deserted, but we were cautious, creeping from tree to tree with our swords in hand.

I led the way, my footsteps soft on the paving

stones, my gaze darting left and right. Hana was next with Manabu beside her, and Tatsuya followed. We slowed our pace as we drew nearer to the end of the pathway. The main street stretched out before us, long and straight, full of eerie shadows.

All the stall-holders had packed up and gone home. There were no signs of the town guards, but they had to be nearby. Lanterns glowed in doorways, and the smell of roasted tea leaves drifted on the air. I lingered in the temple entrance for a moment, listening and watching. Then I glanced back at the others and gave a quick nod. 'Come on,' I said. 'Let's hurry.'

All our senses were alert as we moved swiftly and silently through the town, heading for the gateway, and the path that would take us back out onto the mountainside. The wind seemed to pick up, snuffing out one or two of the iron lanterns which hung at intervals along the street. Away to the north, a dog barked. Closer, I caught the faint sound of someone strumming on a *koto* harp. Once, an old woman's face appeared by a half-open screen, peering out at us.

We were almost at the town gates when a sudden movement in a side alley caught my eye. There was a gleam of lantern-light on burnished steel, and a pair of glittering black eyes stared out from beneath a samurai helmet.

Please, I prayed to the Buddha. *Please don't let him see us. Make us invisible . . .*

But then a rough shout tore the air and I knew that we had been spotted.

Two patrolling soldiers burst out of the shadows, hands on the hilts of their long curved swords.

'Run!' I cried.

chapter 12

We raced away, down the street towards the town gates.

'Into the trees,' I gasped to the others. 'We should be able to lose them in the pine forest!'

Clutching my sword tightly, I risked a glance back over my shoulder—and saw that the two patrolling soldiers had become six . . . and there were more behind them! Eight samurai came swarming out of shadow-filled side alleys like angry hornets. All of them wore Uncle's distinctive red silk *mon* badges. Their leader let out a fierce battle cry as he sprinted after us, leather armour creaking, sword in hand.

But already we were through the town gates! Veering to the left, we made for the trees. Pine needles crunched beneath our feet and branches tore at our clothes as we ran. Then . . . *thunk!* An arrow hit the tree beside me, barely missing my shoulder. I pushed onwards, panting now.

'We've got to get away!' Hana gasped.

'We should go up,' Tatsuya said, 'into the trees.'

'But Manabu can't climb!' I reminded him. 'He's only got one arm.'

'I'm sorry,' Tatsuya said, casting Manabu an embarrassed glance. 'I forgot.'

Manabu waved him away.

'We can help Manabu,' Hana said, coming to an abrupt halt beneath a tall, thick pine tree.

I rammed my sword back into its scabbard and pushed back my sleeves. 'You first,' I said to Hana. 'We'll pull Manabu up behind us.'

Together we shinned up into the ancient tree, found a firm foothold, and then leaned back down to help the manservant. 'Hurry,' Hana urged. 'I can hear the soldiers coming.'

Manabu and I locked a hand around each other's wrists. He climbed quickly, using his feet like a monkey while I bore his weight. Hana reached down and grasped him beneath the armpit, hauling up with all her strength. Her hair had come loose, and it swung like a length of black rope over one shoulder as she leaned down.

A crashing sound carried towards us through the forest, and a hoarse shout reverberated through the pine-scented gloom.

'Hurry, Tatsuya,' I whispered. 'They're so close.'

Tatsuya's face appeared just below Manabu's left foot. 'Higher,' he whispered back, his face tense. 'We need to go higher!'

Hastily we climbed further up into the tree. Branches swayed above my head, trembling and dipping beneath our weight. Far below, I heard the soldiers coming through the ancient forest. They were moving slowly, stealthily, their weapons at the ready.

I caught a glimpse of the leader, his finger to his lips. 'Slowly, slowly,' he said in a low, husky voice. 'Let them think we've lost them. They're only youngsters; they'll soon give themselves away.'

I counted them as they crept by, their sandals soft on the pine needle carpet. One. Two. Three. Four. Five. Six.

Suddenly I noticed Tatsuya. He was crouching on a branch a little way below me, his weight perfectly held in balance.

Slowly, he steadied his longbow, fitted an arrow, took aim . . . and loosed.

The arrow flickered through the air, silent and deadly, aiming straight for the samurai warrior who was bringing up the rear. The arrow took out his throat. For a moment he clawed the air, mouth open. Then he pitched sideways. He was dead before he hit the ground and his friends hadn't even noticed.

Tatsuya loosed a second arrow. It sliced through the air and found a barely visible gap in a samurai's armour, where shoulder-guard met breastplate. The tip buried deep. The samurai pitched forward, but he crashed into the samurai in front of him, alerting the others.

A third soldier backed away from his comrades, looking around for the source of the arrows. In the gathering darkness, his face looked as pale as a bloated fish belly. 'Demons are walking the earth tonight,' he said with a shaky voice.

'Stay together, men,' the leader warned. 'We must find them!'

But I could see that his sword hand was shaking as he disappeared into the gloom. His men hurried after him, vanishing like the spirits they feared.

'Is it safe to go down?' Manabu asked in a low voice.

'Only if you *want* them to catch you,' Tatsuya

said, giving the servant a sharp glance as he flung his longbow onto his shoulder.

'Let's stay up here in the trees,' Hana said in a soothing voice. 'The branches are so close together that we could travel from one to the next with no trouble. Then we'll be out of sight if the soldiers cross our path again.'

I tested a nearby branch with my foot, found it was stable, and nodded. 'Good idea, Hana.'

As dusk turned to night around us, we moved through the tree tops quickly. We made good progress, taking turns to help Manabu. Branches dipped and swayed gracefully beneath our toes as we leaped from one tree to the next. The palms of my hands became sticky with sap. I wondered what we must look like from the ground, with the pale sleeves of our kimono jackets fluttering. If any of the samurai had glanced up and seen us, flitting from branch to branch, they would have thought we were indeed demons, haunting the ancient forest.

Two birds flapped up and away, startled by our presence in the trees. A breeze picked up, whispering through the pine needles, and my mind turned towards Mother and Moriyasu, hiding at the eastern lake. Were they safe there now that night had fallen? Was there shelter to keep them warm and dry? Would we really be able to find them?

'Do you know where on the lake the mistress will be, Kimi-*gozen*?' Manabu asked, almost as if he had been able to read my thoughts.

'I have no idea,' I said. He gave me a sympathetic look. 'My hope is that things will become clear when we get there.'

A soft rain had begun to fall, making the branches slippery and treacherous, especially for Manabu. He stepped past me, his feet easing along a wet branch in search of firmer footing. Suddenly he slipped. I shot out a hand and gripped his sleeve, twisting him back up to safety.

'Thank you, Kimi-*gozen*,' the servant said. 'I am so sorry to hold you back . . .'

'The soldiers are long gone,' Tatsuya said. 'Perhaps it would be all right for Manabu to be let down from the tree now?' He glanced at the way ahead. 'We're almost at the edge of the forest anyway.'

I knew that Tatsuya felt that Manabu was a burden. We were moving more slowly than we would have done if the servant hadn't been with us. But Mother had sent him to us, and we couldn't abandon him.

'We must stay together,' I told Tatsuya firmly.

Manabu smiled at me and moved on into the next tree. Hana followed him, her arms spread wide as she kept her centre of balance. The moon was beginning to rise, and the silver light picked out the raindrops sparkling in her dark hair.

The trees were further apart as we neared the edge of the forest and we couldn't climb between them easily. Ahead I could see the moon, half full, sitting low over the rocky mountainside, its light glinting on the lake we could see that stretched out like a black mirror far below. We could only see this one lake, as the others were each visible from different points on the enormous mountain.

Hana was crouching on a nearby branch, peering towards the ground. 'Is it safe to go down?' she asked.

We all held our breath, listening and looking. There seemed to be no sign of any soldiers, but Tatsuya put his fingers to his lips to signal that we should be quiet while he checked.

He shinned down the tree and dropped to the ground, landing softly on a carpet of wet pine needles. He edged forward and scanned the moonlit landscape, then did a small circuit of the last few shadowy trees, just to be sure.

Eventually he signalled up to us. All clear!

Hana and I helped Manabu out of the trees. We

brushed ourselves down and I picked a small pine cone from Hana's hair. Then we struck out towards the east, keeping the mountain behind us. We walked in a line, one behind the other with Manabu in the lead, then Hana, then Tatsuya, and then me. I kept my head down against the rain, counting my footsteps as they squelched in the mud.

Ahead of me, I could hear Hana and Manabu talking about the uprising, and the way Uncle Hidehira's men had begun the slaughter.

'What happened to you that night, Manabu?' Hana asked gently. 'Kimi and I believed that everyone had been killed.'

'Many people were,' Manabu said, his voice bitter. 'Hidehira ordered a massacre . . . ' He glanced back over his shoulder and I caught a glimpse of his thin face, bleak memories etched across it. 'I was in the servants' quarters when I heard the first screams. I rushed to the mistress's room to warn her. She wanted to run and help your father, but I persuaded her that it would be too dangerous. I helped her bundle up young Moriyasu-*gozen*, and the three of us escaped together. I have been helping them ever since, arranging for the delivery of letters to Master Goku and keeping watch for soldiers.'

'How is Moriyasu?' I asked. 'He must have been so frightened.' My soul twisted at the thought.

Manabu shot me a sympathetic look. 'He is his father's son, and very brave. The two of them cannot wait to see you again.'

My heart swelled with love at the thought of Moriyasu being so brave.

'And what about you two?' Manabu asked Hana. 'Life must have been very difficult for you both. You were lucky to find people to help you while you were in hiding.' He glanced at me with a friendly smile. 'They say there are rebel groups preparing a rebellion against the new *jito* . . . perhaps you know them already?'

I shook my head. 'I've heard of them,' I said, remembering what the priest at the temple had told us. 'But we don't know who they are. It was difficult work at the *dojo*, as servants, but we learned so much from Master Goku and we will be for ever grateful to him for his kindness.'

'You were lucky to stumble on such a friend,' Manabu said.

I nodded, feeling the loss of my Master yet again.

Soon the rain eased off, and finally stopped altogether. I straightened up and looked around, catching a glimpse of the lake. We'd come a long way. Behind us, the forest was now no more than a dark line on the horizon.

During our walk I noticed Tatsuya glancing back over his shoulder several times, as if he thought someone was following us. I caught up to him and touched his sleeve. 'Are you all right?' I asked him in a low voice.

He hesitated, and then said, 'I don't want to worry you,' he said reluctantly, 'but I think there might be someone tracking us.'

My heart missed a beat. 'Are you sure?'

He nodded.

Up ahead, Manabu had come to a halt. He gave Tatsuya a doubtful glance. 'Surely you're imagining things, young master,' he said.

Tatsuya bristled and was about to argue when Hana spoke up. 'I feel it too,' she said, her gaze fixed on some faraway point in the darkness behind us. 'There is someone close by.'

I shivered, feeling suddenly cold and vulnerable out on the open mountainside. 'We should make sure,' I said, glancing around warily. 'Let's double back . . . stay hidden . . . '

Tatsuya caught my gaze and nodded. 'Good idea,' he said. 'If we circle back towards the forest, then whoever is following will be ahead of us. We'll come up behind them.'

I nodded, and Tatsuya silently led us off the path. With Hana and Manabu following cautiously behind, we made our way behind a craggy outcrop and away across the mountainside. Above us, the rain clouds thickened again, almost obscuring the half-moon.

At last we curved back towards our own pathway. Tatsuya crouched down to peer at the tracks in the mud.

I leaned over his shoulder and saw our own footprints—Hana's and mine small, Tatsuya's slightly larger, and Manabu's those of a full-grown man. But there were also others—large prints, like Manabu's, that obliterated the traces of ours here and there.

'Some of those footprints are on top of ours and others are to the side,' Hana whispered. 'They could only have been made since we passed this way.'

We looked around, eyes straining against the darkness, but there was no sign of anyone nearby.

'Who do you think it is?' Manabu asked anxiously.

'It must be Uncle's soldiers,' I said, as I turned a full circle, scanning the rocks and shadows, the bushes and occasional straggly tree. I could see no one, but the skin prickled on the back of my neck as I wondered whether *they* could see *me*.

'What shall we do, Kimi?' whispered Hana, looking into my eyes with concern on her face.

'We have to lose them,' I told her. 'Because if we don't, we'll lead them right to Mother and Moriyasu!'

164

Chapter 13

Determined to confuse the soldiers and throw them off our track, we took a deviating trail across the mountain.

A couple of times, we doubled back again, hoping to find only our own footprints in the mud. But on every occasion my heart sank like a stone dropped into a pond—we always saw those same prints, obliterating our own.

Hana looked around, her gaze probing every contour of the mountainside. 'Why don't we ever see the soldiers who are making these prints?' she asked.

'Because it's their turn to be like demons,' I said grimly.

Tatsuya looked grave. Perhaps he thought it was ninja again.

Even as we stood at the side of the track, looking down, the rain began to fall again, heavier this time. It quickly washed the footprints away, and filled the ruts in the track until they became small lakes. I watched our tracks disappear, and bit my lip thoughtfully. There must be some way to avoid making fresh footprints.

Glancing around, I saw a tumble of rocks nearby.

'We should climb up on there,' I said. 'We won't leave prints on the rock, and any disturbance we make, or signs of our passing, will be washed away by the rain.'

'Good idea,' Tatsuya said.

We scrambled up, fingers and sandals sliding on the wet surface. Some of the rocks shifted dangerously under our weight, but even so we felt safer up there. We hurried along, heads down against the rain. I was cold and tired. Rain plastered my hair to my face. Then one of Hana's frayed sandals broke, and I knew we should stop.

'We can shelter up there,' Tatsuya said, pointing to a rocky overhang.

We scrambled up and squeezed together, grateful to be out of the rain at last. Tatsuya said he would keep watch, while I tore a strip of cloth from the inside of my kimono and fixed Hana's sandal as best I could. Her feet were icy to the touch, and I reflected for a moment on how much our lives had changed since the golden days at the *shinden* when our maids would have rubbed our feet with pumice stone to soften them, and then bathed them in scented oils.

Hana must have guessed what I was thinking, because she caught my eye and we exchanged a sad, secret look. 'Our old life seems so far away, doesn't it?' she said gently. 'But one day soon, everything will come right again, Kimi.'

The rain worsened. A chill wind howled across the mountainside. Wet and cold, we huddled together in the darkness for warmth. Beyond the rocky overhang, the rain tipped out of the black sky like thin bamboo rods.

After a while, Manabu put his head on his knees and seemed to sleep. Tatsuya crouched with his swords across his lap, gaze fixed on the dark horizon as he watched for soldiers. Hana rested against my shoulder. Soon her breathing slowed and I knew she was sleeping.

I closed my eyes and felt my mind drift into that place where sleep hovers. Time stretched around me, and after a while I dreamed of standing in a garden. Mother was there, holding an open scroll in her hands and smiling as she read the poem about the five lakes to me. I felt my heart soar at the sight of her, but when I tried to hurry across the garden towards her I found I couldn't move. I called out, but Mother turned her face away, and when I awoke my cheeks were wet with tears.

I sat still, half awake, shivering in the cold. It was still raining. Hana snuggled closer to me and I put my arm around her, wondering how long the storm would go on. I pictured Mother, waiting for us, worrying and wondering why we did not come. I thought about how she had recited the poem in my dream. How beautiful it had been to hear her voice again, and to listen to the words of the poem. Fujigoko. Five lakes. Five elements. Wood and fire, metal and water, earth . . .

Suddenly I sat up straight and clutched Hana's sleeve. 'I know what Mother meant!' I exclaimed, and Hana woke with a start. 'We must find a place on the lake that has all five of the elements. Water and earth are there already . . . but she means that we should find somewhere near the water, with wood, metal, and fire as well!'

Hana's eyes focused on me and then lit up with excitement. '*Wood, Fire, Earth, Metal, Water,*' she recited, fully awake now. *'Nothing can break the strength of all five elements when they are together.'*

'Let's go now,' I said. 'I don't care about the rain. Now that we know what to look for, I want to get there as quickly as possible!'

'It looks as if the rain is slowing now anyway,' Tatsuya said as he stood up. It surprised me that he was already awake. Was it our excitement that had stirred him?

Hana reached out as if to shake Manabu awake, but he lifted his head before she could touch him. The servant looked startled for a moment and reached for his blade as if he had forgotten where he was. Then his shoulders relaxed and he laughed. 'I've slept in many strange places, Hana-*gozen*,' he said. 'But never under a rock. We've turned into beetles, eh?'

Hana and I exchanged an amused look, and Hana hid her smile behind her hand. I grinned across at Tatsuya, but he didn't grin back. He seemed different—wary and watchful—and I wondered whether he had slept at all.

'We're almost at the end of our journey,' I said, watching him check his arrows.

'I hope so,' he murmured, his expression blank.

I wouldn't let him spoil my excitement.

Everything was going to work out all right—Hana and I were nearly there!

I was filled with new energy as we set off down the mountainside. There was no sign of anyone following us and I felt sure we had lost whoever it had been.

'Things are beginning to go our way,' I said to Hana as we walked.

She nodded and smiled. 'We know where we're going, and we seem to have lost the soldiers.'

'The rain has stopped, too,' Tatsuya observed.

Soon the rain clouds broke apart and moonlight bathed the landscape once more. Silvery beams picked up rocks and bushes . . . and away in the distance, far below, a great expanse of water that gleamed like black onyx.

'There's the eastern lake,' Hana said.

We hurried on, making our way ever faster downhill. The ground became steep, and so wet that it was treacherous in parts. I slipped and slid, and when the rain began to come down again I thought I would weep with frustration. We hit a bank of thick mud which clung to our sandals and oozed around our feet. Quickly I bent down and rolled up the bottoms of my trousers, tying them at the back.

'This mud is like glue,' Hana said, who was just

behind me. We were walking single file, heads down, with Manabu in the lead and Tatsuya bringing up the rear.

Manabu suddenly stopped, holding his arm out to make everyone halt behind him. 'I don't think we should go any further,' he said uncertainly. 'This doesn't feel right.'

I looked down and saw that the mud came up to my knees, swirling like soup. I glanced back at Hana and saw that she was up to her ankles.

'This isn't ordinary mud,' I said, my heart suddenly hammering against my ribs. 'It's more like quicksand . . . '

Ahead of me, Manabu began to struggle, then sank even deeper into the mud. 'I can't lift my foot!'

Tatsuya was behind us, and called out, 'Don't make any sudden movements. Just relax. The more you struggle, the faster you will sink.'

'I'm frightened,' Hana said.

Tatsuya was close enough to reach out and take her hand. 'You haven't gone as deep as the others,' he said. 'Move slowly towards me . . . '

Hana glanced at me and I nodded. 'Do as he says,' I urged breathlessly. I could feel the mud tight around my knees, a cold and deadly vice.

Slowly, Hana lifted first one foot and then the

next, moving back towards the firmer ground. The mud made sucking sounds as she reached Tatsuya, but it let her go.

Manabu, meanwhile, was struggling. And sinking deeper. 'It's pulling me under!' he cried.

Tatsuya shook his head. 'No,' he said firmly. 'Don't panic, Manabu. It's just water and earth.'

'How do you know?' Manabu's movements had slowed, but he was still struggling a little.

'I've been caught like this before,' Tatsuya explained, as he gently guided Hana to safer ground. 'Out in the marshes near my village. So you're going to listen and do as I say. Keep still and listen to me.'

When Hana was safe, Tatsuya turned back to look at me. 'Kimi, try to lie down,' he ordered.

'Lie down?' I repeated uncertainly.

Tatsuya nodded. 'Trust me,' he said, fixing me with his intense gaze. 'Standing up means all your weight will go down through your feet, and you'll sink more quickly, whereas if you lie down, your body area will be bigger. That makes it harder to sink.' He glanced at Manabu. 'You both need to lie down on the mud.'

I glanced at Manabu. His eyes were wide with fear, but he nodded and I took a deep breath. I bent my knees and slowly lowered myself further down into the cold, wet mud. It squelched and sucked loudly, oozing around me. For a moment I thought that Tatsuya was wrong, and that the mud was going to swallow me. Then suddenly I realized I seemed to be floating on top of the mud, like a lily on a pond.

I glanced at Manabu and saw that he was flat on his stomach, his arm and both his legs spread wide.

'What do we do now?' I asked, turning my face to the side so that I didn't take a mouthful of the mud.

Tatsuya crouched down, a short distance away. 'Stretch out your arm,' he urged. 'Take my hand!'

I stretched out. Our fingertips didn't quite touch.

'I'll find a branch or something for you to hold on to!' Hana said quickly. She darted away towards a clump of trees.

Manabu made a whimpering sound. I turned to look at him. Had he sunk a little lower in the mud? His chin was black, and he was straining to tilt his head back and keep his face free.

'Help him!' I said, panicking. 'He's going to drown!'

A muscle twitched in Tatsuya's jaw. 'He won't drown,' he said sharply. He stretched his arm out further to me. 'Come on, Kimi! Reach for my hand.'

Manabu made a gurgling sound, his eyes widening.

'Help him first!' I cried desperately to Tatsuya. 'He's sinking!'

'He's not sinking,' Tatsuya insisted. 'He's fine for a few moments. I want to get you out first.'

I remembered how much Tatsuya disliked Manabu. Surely he didn't mean to let him drown? I glanced at Tatsuya's fingers, stretching towards me, and quickly snatched mine back. 'Help Manabu first,' I said flatly.

Tatsuya's dark eyes met mine. 'Only when you're safe, Kimi,' he said. 'Give me your hand.'

'No,' I said, tears of frustration welling in my eyes. 'You help Manabu. Please. He's one of the last survivors of my father's household . . . help him for my sake.'

Tatsuya muttered something beneath his breath and glanced over his shoulder to see if Hana was coming. But she was nowhere to be seen, lost among the shadowy clump of trees where she searched for a branch.

Tatsuya turned back and gave me one last, long look and then quickly shrugged off his longbow and arrows. Tossing the arrows aside, he spread himself flat on the mud and reached the longbow out towards Manabu. 'Grab this!' he said to the servant. 'And hold on tight. I'm going to pull you out.'

My heart in my mouth, I watched as Tatsuya strained against the mud which threatened to engulf Manabu. I could feel it soaking up through my *hakama* trousers, cold and wet and clinging, almost sucking at me. For a moment, hopelessness came over me in waves. We were so close to Mother. So close. And yet again we could not reach her.

Hana is safe, I thought. *She can tell Mother that I tried . . . Manabu will keep her safe . . .*

I heard Tatsuya grunt, and then Manabu cried out. With a huge sucking sound, he came free. Relief swept through me as I saw him grasp Tatsuya's wrist with his one hand, and Tatsuya was dragging him away, both of them stumbling, limbs half entwined as they staggered to the edge of the mud patch where Manabu collapsed, panting.

At that moment, Hana came running back with a long, sturdy branch in her hand. She threw herself onto her knees at the edge of the mud patch. 'Grab hold of this, Kimi!'

I felt muddy water seeping up around my chin

as I stretched out towards the branch. But I couldn't reach it! I strained forward. My legs were stuck. The mud seemed to have a life of its own, dragging me down, setting like hard clay around my knees.

All at once, my own limbs gave a squelching popping sound—and then I was free! The mud sloshed around me, gurgling greedily, but Tatsuya had me by my kimono. He pulled, and Hana grabbed my arm, and together the three of us half stumbled, half crawled to where Manabu was lying.

'Buddha be praised,' I said, weak with relief as I hugged Hana.

Manabu looked up at Tatsuya. 'Thank you,' he said. 'You saved my life.'

Tatsuya nodded curtly but said nothing. I tried to catch his eye to say my own thanks, but he avoided my gaze.

'We shouldn't stay here,' Hana warned, glancing up at the heavy sky. 'If the rains come again, we could be caught once more.'

'Let's try and make it over to that rock,' Manabu suggested, pointing.

'Good idea,' I said. 'It's nice and high. We can climb up onto it and try to get an idea of the safest way around this mud.'

With mud clotting our hair and clothes, we picked our way carefully to the rock. Breathless, we hauled ourselves up onto it.

Hana reached out to help Manabu, and then turned to look at me, her face suddenly full of laughter. Mud was smeared across her cheeks and chin.

'Earlier I thought I'd seen enough rain for a lifetime,' she said, turning her hands over and examining her black palms. 'But now I pray for rain again to wash us clean!'

I scrambled to my feet and looked in the direction of the lake. The half-moon was bright now, lighting a silver path across the water all the way to the far side. 'We're almost there,' I said to Hana. 'We can bathe in the lake, and rinse our clothes and hair.'

She nodded, and stood up beside me, her fingers lightly touching mine in our secret signal of kinship. 'Mother is there somewhere,' she said, then her gaze sharpened. 'Look, Kimi, can you see that enormous boulder at the edge of the lake, next to that tree stump? That could be three of the elements—earth, wood, and water.'

I nodded. 'But what about the fire and metal? I can't see any smoke, or houses, or even any signs of life.'

Tatsuya tilted his mud-smeared face up to the sky. 'It will be dawn soon,' he said. 'We may be able to see more in the daylight.'

Manabu nodded. 'We should head towards the boulder,' he said. 'Perhaps there's something beyond it that we cannot see from here?' He glanced at me and smiled. 'We might be lucky enough to find a village where there are people who can help us.'

Soon we came to the shoreline. A chill mist curled up from the lake. I heard the soft lap of water as a fish jumped. As we got closer, dawn's early light streaked across the sky.

I saw it then—a ledge of red stone slicing across the otherwise grey boulder.

'There!' I said breathlessly, pointing. 'That red stone must signify fire!'

We hurried onwards, following the shoreline as the morning dawned around us. A clear, crisp, pale light washed colour into the landscape. Birds began to wheel across the sky, and somewhere a couple of frogs rasped their song.

When we reached the boulder, I saw that there was a streak of something silvery in the red stone. 'Metal,' I said, turning to Hana. 'The last of the elements!'

I put out one hand and placed it flat on the

surface, feeling the cool smooth hardness beneath my palm. A feeling of peace and serenity stole over me.

Hana sank to her knees beside me. 'Mother has been here,' she said softly. 'I'm sure of it!'

'But where is she now?' I asked impatiently. We had been journeying for so long, surely we were at the end . . .

Looking as if she was in a trance, Hana bent forward in a formal *seiza* position then bowed low, her fingers pointing together and almost touching. After a moment she sat back in *seiza* again, her face looking as beautiful as the flowers she had been named for. 'We have come to the right place, Kimi,' she said.

As she glanced up at me I saw a sparkle of tears in her dark eyes. But they were tears of happiness, because she was smiling.

'What is it, Hana?' I asked, kneeling beside her.

Still smiling, she leaned forward to reach beneath the ledge of red stone.

Behind us, Tatsuya rested his hand on the scabbard of his sword and came to stand next to Manabu. Both were silent as they watched Hana's hands move from side to side. She was feeling for something . . . searching beneath the ledge.

At last her hands were still for a moment. Then she drew out a beautiful black lacquered box.

'Kimi . . . ' she whispered.

My heart almost stopped beating as I looked down at the box in her hands. The Yamamoto symbol was carved into the lid . . .

I knew at once that Mother had left it here for us to find.

chapter 14

Hana cupped the box in both hands and offered it to me. 'It must contain another message,' she whispered.

Trembling with excitement, I took the black lacquered box from Hana's hands and carefully lifted the lid. A delicate scent drifted out and was carried up to my nose on the clear, crisp morning air.

Cherry blossom. Mother's favourite perfume. And inside the box was a single twig of a cherry blossom tree.

I lifted the branch out slowly and held it up to try and catch the first rays of daylight.

'Isn't there anything else in the box?' Hana

asked, her face puzzled. 'No letter . . . no paper scroll . . . ?'

I shook my head. 'Just the cherry blossom branch.'

We checked the box thoroughly, to make sure there was no letter concealed beneath a false bottom or stuck into the lid. But there was nothing. I held the slender branch in my hand and stared at it. Mother was sending us a message, but her meaning was closed to me.

'It's a mystery,' Hana murmured. She looked around at the shadowy shores of the lake. 'If there were cherry blossom trees around here, it might make some sense—perhaps it might be a pointer to another clue.' She gently took the branch from me and turned it over in her fingers. 'But this is just a piece from a cherry blossom tree.'

My shoulders sagged and exhaustion suddenly washed over me. Mother seemed as far away as she ever had. I was cold, tired, covered with mud, and close to tears.

Hana must have seen the expression on my face, because she gently took the lacquered box from my hands and put the twig away. She handed the box to Tatsuya and slipped her hand into mine.

'Come, Kimi,' she said quietly. 'Come down to

the water with me. We'll wash off some of the mud.'

We left Tatsuya and Manabu, who hunkered down at a wary distance from each other. Both of them appeared to be keeping lookout; Manabu closely scrutinizing the shoreline while Tatsuya kept checking over his shoulder.

Down at the edge of the lake, I scooped up handfuls of cool clear water and began to wash my hands. Hana pulled her hair out of the top-knot, bent forward, and swept her long hair over one shoulder, slowly rinsing it clean of mud. I had a brief flash of memory—our wooden bath house at home, filled with clouds of hot steam.

Hana's voice broke into my thoughts. 'We've come so far, Kimi,' she said. 'I can't bear to think that we might be defeated now.'

'I don't think Mother would have left something that was too obscure,' I said thoughtfully. 'There must be something that we've missed.'

Hana nodded, squeezing a stream of silvery-blue water from her hair. She looked tired, and I realized that apart from our brief sleep during the storm we had had no real rest since we'd left the inn.

'It's not yet full daylight,' I said as we made our way back up the shore to the others. 'Why don't we settle down for a while? You can get some sleep while I try to figure things out.'

Hana nodded gratefully as she twisted her wet hair up into a top-knot and secured it tightly. She leaned up against the red rock, closed her eyes, and seemed to sink quickly into sleep. I sat beside Tatsuya, holding the lacquered box in my hands, idly opening and closing its lid as I willed the box to give up its secrets.

Soon, I was too tired to stay awake any longer. I propped the lacquered box in the grass beside me and lay down beside Hana, exhausted. I dreamed of Master Goku.

I was back in the Meditation Room at the *dojo*, fragrant incense hanging on the air. Master Goku walked towards me across the polished floor, almost gliding, his black robes rippling around his bare feet. His gaze rested on my face for a moment.

'Steady your mind, Kimi,' he said. 'Steel your heart.'

I awoke with a jolt. Beside me, Tatsuya was resting his head back against the rock behind him, eyes closed. Manabu had walked down to the water's edge. He had picked up a stick and was using it to make swirling shapes in the half-dried mud.

I became aware of Hana beside me. Her dark eyes were open and she was looking at me.

'I'm sorry,' I whispered. 'Did I wake you?'

'I had a dream,' she whispered back. 'I saw Goku.' Her face clouded. 'We were in the Meditation Room and he told me to steel my heart.'

'I had the same dream,' I said, knowing that it must mean something powerful. I reached over and squeezed my sister's hand. 'That's what woke me.'

I sat up and pushed a loose strand of hair back from my face.

The lacquered box was still propped in the grass beside me, and something caught my eye—a shimmer of light and a pearl of moisture. The swirling mist coming up from the lake had left a trail of condensation across the outside of the lacquered lid.

I frowned and lifted the box, looking closer.

Beads of moisture from the swirling mist had formed around a shape on the lid. A *kanji* shape! Excitement rushed through me as I realized Mother must have smeared some kind of oil on the lacquer to make a message.

'Look, Hana!' I whispered. 'There's a message . . . '

Hana stared at the lacquered box. 'What does it say?'

I studied the *kanji* for a moment. '*Safe house,*' I read aloud, '*is where river meets lake.*'

I looked up, across the lake. The sun was rising quickly now, flashing off the water and making a thousand tiny diamond shapes which sparkled and danced. The mist rose like steam clouds, and far away on the far side of the smooth water I could just make out the mouth of a wide river, and a cluster of rooftops which looked like a small town.

'There!' I said, pointing. 'That's where Mother's safe house is.'

Tatsuya stirred beside me, blinking and frowning. 'Sorry,' he said. 'I must have fallen asleep for a moment. What's going on?'

Manabu, hearing our voices, dropped his stick and started to walk back towards us. His face was full of concern. 'Is everything all right?' he asked.

'Kimi has found a message from Mother,' Hana told them both, her eyes shining with happiness. 'There's a safe house on the other side of the lake!'

Tatsuya shaded his eyes with his hand. 'It could take a while to walk all the way around there,' he said with a frown. 'Perhaps half a day.'

My heart sank. There had to be another way. 'What about a boat?'

Manabu looked from me to Hana and back again. 'I thought I saw a fishing village a little further along the shore,' he said, pointing past the big overhang of rock. 'The early sunlight picked up a few rooftops. It doesn't look much, just a handful of tiny hovels . . . but maybe we could get some food there, and one of the fishermen might have a boat he would lend us.'

I grinned. 'What are we waiting for?'

It was a short walk around the shoreline to the village.

I could see two small flat boats pulled up on the mud in front of the cluster of hovels. One boat looked rickety but the other looked as though it might make it across the lake. Beside them sat a fisherman wearing a faded blue jacket and ragged trousers. His thin hands were tangled among the folds of a fishing net. He looked up from under bushy eyebrows as we approached. I gave him a friendly smile and stepped forward.

'Kimi-*gozen*,' Manabu said, gently touching my sleeve. 'While you talk to this man, perhaps I should go and see whether the villagers will let us have some food?' He made a wry face as he patted his stomach. 'It's a long time since any of us have eaten.'

'That's a good idea,' I said, fishing for the pouch of coins I'd taken from the innkeeper. 'Here—take this.'

Manabu took the pouch, bowed, and hurried away.

With Hana and Tatsuya one step behind me, I turned back to the fisherman.

'What do you want?' he asked, eyeing me warily.

I made a formal bow. To show the utmost respect, I placed my hands flat to my thighs and turned my fingertips inwards until they almost touched. 'We are on our way to the little town at the mouth of the river,' I explained politely. 'It's such a long way to walk. We wondered if you might have a boat we could borrow, to reach the other side of the lake?'

'You think I'd lend my boat to strangers?' The fisherman snorted. 'My boat is my livelihood. If you don't bring it back, then I don't fish. And if I don't fish, then my family doesn't eat.'

Hana crouched down in front of the fisherman. 'Perhaps you could row us across the lake yourself,' she suggested. 'Then you would be able to bring the boat back afterwards.'

'Why should I do that?' the fisherman demanded. 'I'm a busy man. I don't have time to go jaunting across the lake on a pleasure trip!'

Hana looked up at me. I hesitated for a moment and then held out the beautiful lacquered box. 'We would pay you,' I said. 'You can have this box; it must be worth something.'

The fisherman raised his eyebrows. 'My family can't eat a box,' he said bitterly. 'I don't know where you travellers have come from, but in these parts there's a food shortage.' He jerked his chin at me.

I bit my lip, realizing that Uncle Hidehira's iron grip must have reached even the Fujigoko lakes. 'I'm sorry,' I said.

'Sorry?' the fisherman tutted. 'What are you sorry for, eh? It's not your fault that my children are starving and my wife is ill!' With a grunt, he turned back to his nets.

I crouched down beside Hana. 'There is still hope for the land,' I said gently. 'There are many people who want to see an end to Lord Hidehira's reign.'

The fisherman refused to look at me. 'I don't know about that,' he muttered, his fingers moving quickly in the folds of his net. 'I've said too much already . . . how do I know you aren't travellers but spies for the *jito*, eh? Maybe you've been sent to trap me with words.'

I shook my head. 'We're not spies,' I said, deciding to take a risk. If we were to borrow a boat and get to Mother, we had to persuade this man to trust us. 'Too many people who were dear to us have been killed by Lord Hidehira. As long as we live we'll be fighting *against* him—not *for* him.'

The fisherman's hands fell still. He glanced up at me. 'Are you with the rebels?' he asked quietly.

I nodded.

A look of relief passed across his face. 'And you want to go across the lake . . . to meet others who disagree with the new *jito*'s policies?'

I nodded again.

'Then I would be honoured to row you across to the other side,' the fisherman said.

I held out the lacquered box, but he shook his head.

'I will take you for the good of the kingdom,' he said firmly. 'Not because I want payment.'

'Please,' I insisted. 'The box is yours.'

The fisherman reluctantly took the box in gnarled hands. 'In that case, perhaps you will honour me by taking a bowl of something with my family. I can't offer much more than soup, but it would do my wife good to see your faces and know that there is hope.'

I glanced at Hana and Tatsuya, who both nodded.

Manabu rejoined us just as we were following the fisherman to his hut. 'These people are starving,' the servant said quietly as he handed the innkeeper's coins back to me. 'They don't have any food to sell.'

'That's all right,' I said, and quickly told him that the fisherman wanted to give us bowls of soup.

Manabu nodded approvingly, and used his hand to usher us all ahead of him. Ducking our heads, we stepped through the screen door and entered the fisherman's hut. The place smelt strongly of fish and looked as if it had been built from bits of timber found on the shore. Inside, a little girl of about Moriyasu's age was stirring an iron pot. A woman was tucked into a low futon bed in one corner. She looked thin and pale, and I guessed she was the fisherman's wife. Two tiny children huddled at the foot of the bed. They stared at us as we came in, their eyes huge and round.

At a word from the fisherman, the little girl scooped watery soup into roughly-carved wooden bowls and handed it around. Watched by the fisherman, his wife, and their children, we sipped at the soup. It was mostly water, with a few ragged pieces of fish skin floating in it.

My soul ached to see how generous and dignified these people were, even though they were dressed in rags and had nothing but wooden bowls to eat from. Silently, I swore that when Uncle's reign came to an end I would make sure that these people were treated fairly, as they had been when my father had been *jito*.

Anger burned in my heart at the thought of Uncle so quickly destroying Father's work. Until now I had been consumed with the desire for vengeance, and a desperate need to restore the honour of my family name. But standing in that tiny hovel with a shaft of early morning light slanting through a gap in the timbers, I realized there was more to it than that. It wasn't just Father and my brothers that I had to avenge. It was every starving fisherman and every poor rice farmer, too.

When we had finished eating, we said goodbye to the wife and children and made our way back to the shoreline. I knelt beside Hana in the bottom of the boat and tried to contain my excitement. We were so nearly there! As Manabu and Tatsuya settled opposite us, I caught Hana's eye.

'I can't wait to see Moriyasu,' I said.

'And Mother,' she said, taking a deep, calming breath. 'We have come so far, Kimi.'

I nodded. 'But there's even further to go,' I murmured. 'Mother will want to gather the rebels together. Raise an army. Fight against Uncle!'

Manabu nodded and gave us a beaming look, but Tatsuya avoided my eye. He seemed thoughtful. What was going on with him? As the boat pulled away from the shore, he kept looking behind him, scanning the hovels.

'I hope we don't have to start fighting just yet,' Hana said. 'I want to spend time with Mother, just being a family again.'

I nodded, and we were both quiet for a while, listening to the plopping of the sculling pole dipping in and out of the water.

As soon as we reached the other side, the fisherman lashed the boat to a wooden post sticking up out of the water.

'I will bid you farewell,' he said, bowing to each of us in turn. 'I hope that one day we meet again, when the tide has turned and the land is once more what it was under Lord Yoshijiro.'

Hana and I bowed low to hide our emotion at the sound of Father's name. 'Thank you,' I said. 'I hope you find a trader to give you a good price for the box.'

We watched him hurry away, and then I turned to take stock of the town.

There were little more than two dozen houses huddled beside the shoreline where the mouth of the river met the lake. A few boats had been pulled up on the mud, and a skinny dog sniffed a pile of fishing nets. It was still early, and the main street was deserted as we made our way along it.

'Where is everyone?' Hana asked in a puzzled voice. 'I expected Mother to be in hiding—but it seems as if the whole town has gone to ground.'

'Perhaps the people are frightened,' I said, catching a glimpse of a pale face in a doorway which quickly disappeared as we drew closer. 'Maybe they think we've been sent by Uncle?'

We came to the outskirts of the town. A spreading maple tree shaded the road which curved away along the riverbank. Nearby was a small hut with a few dusty-looking horses tied up at the rear.

Hana suddenly quickened her pace and went ahead a few steps. 'Look,' she said in a hushed voice, pointing at the bamboo-screened door of the hut. Something was nailed to the door frame. 'Kimi, it's a cherry branch!'

My heart skipped a beat and then began to race with excitement. 'Mother!' I said breathlessly.

'Be careful,' Tatsuya said in a warning voice. 'We don't know that it's safe here.'

With a nod at me to go ahead, Manabu put his hand on the scabbard of his sword.

Together, Hana and I hurried to the hut and I knocked on the door frame. There was no response. I shifted my weight from one foot to the other, feeling impatient. We were so close! Mother and Moriyasu could be just beyond this bamboo screen.

I turned to Hana. 'Shall we go in?' I whispered.

She nodded, her face shining with joy. 'Mother's here,' she said. 'I can almost smell her perfume. Come on, Kimi . . . '

Heart racing, I slid back the screen door and stepped into the hut.

It was almost dark inside, smoky and dimly-lit. There was a charcoal brazier in one corner, and a long low wooden table in the centre of the room. Chopsticks and dirty wooden bowls were littered across the surface. The room smelt of stale rice and vinegar.

At the far end of the table, two figures knelt

silently in the *seiza* position on rough straw mats. Their hands rested lightly on their thighs and their backs were straight. One was a woman, her long hair hanging loose over her shoulder like a rope of exquisite black silk. The other was a little boy with round cheeks.

'Mother! Moriyasu!' I cried joyfully.

Suddenly the days and weeks of tension flooded from my body, leaving me free to rush forward, pulling Hana with me. We were reunited, at last!

Too late, I saw the look of warning flash across my mother's face as five fierce-looking samurai stepped out of the shadows.

196

chapter 15

My heart plunged into the pit of my stomach.

'No!' I cried in desperation, drawing my sword in a sweep of silver steel. Hana was right beside me, her *nihonto* flowing into her hand.

I could hear Tatsuya in the doorway behind us, rounding on Manabu. 'Traitor!' He spat the word through gritted teeth. 'You're the only one who could have told those soldiers where to look!'

Shocked, I twisted around to see that Tatsuya had grabbed Manabu by the front of his kimono and was shaking him like a rat. Everything seemed to be happening in slow motion.

'You sneaked off when you went to find food at

the other village!' Tatsuya said accusingly. 'It must have been a stroke of luck for you when we were all inside that fisherman's hut, and your friends could slip away.'

Tatsuya shoved Manabu out through the doorway and I instinctively took a step to follow. The manservant staggered backwards, lost his balance, and fell into the mud outside.

'Tatsuya!' I cried, hardly able to believe what my friend was doing.

'You *knew* whose footprints those were following us!' Tatsuya shouted.

Flushing red with fury, Manabu scrambled back up onto his knees. His hand flashed to the hilt of his short sword and I thought he was going to attack Tatsuya—

But instead he reached across the front of his own body and slashed through the folded cloth where his left arm should have been. As I watched, an arm uncurled from beneath the fabric. I gasped. The world seemed to tilt around me.

For as long as I had known him, our servant had only had one arm. But there he sat, with two arms, one clutching a shining sword.

Manabu held my shocked gaze, his eyes narrow and black. An evil smile curved across his thin mouth. He had kept his left arm hidden all this time, strapped to his side. For how many moons . . . ? My mind whirled.

Tatsuya turned to me, his face red with anger. 'That man is a traitor,' he said in a hard voice. 'We should have left him to drown in the quicksand!'

Behind him, Manabu sprang nimbly to his feet and leaped at Tatsuya, sword raised.

'Look out!' I yelled.

Tatsuya twisted towards the glinting blade, but it was too late. The manservant grabbed him, thrust the sword to his throat, and shoved him forward so that he stumbled into Hana and me. Hana's *nihonto* went spinning away onto the ground. I struggled to raise my sword, but Manabu saw me and brought the edge of one fist down across my knuckles. His hand was as hard as steel and I cried out in pain.

With brute strength, Manabu bundled us all completely into the hut. I saw that the samurai had their swords in their hands and were grouped around Mother and Moriyasu, their eyes glittering dangerously in the half light.

Mother looked desperate, her agonized gaze darting from my face to Hana's and back again. Moriyasu was trembling, his little hands folded so tightly in his lap that his knuckles gleamed white. A samurai stood over him.

Leave him alone! I wanted to shout.

Manabu snapped the bamboo screen door shut behind him, and then gestured to two of the samurai. 'Strip them of their weapons,' he said in a hard, unfamiliar voice.

The soldiers hurried to do as he commanded, but I was ready. My knuckles still smarted from Manabu's blow, but I held my blade in a steady two-handed grip. I was aware of Tatsuya to my left. Manabu's sword was still trained on his throat, so there was nothing he could do.

It was all down to me, now.

For a moment there was a stand-off. I held the black gaze of the nearest samurai, daring him to step closer. Then Hana's voice cut through the haze of desperation in my mind.

'Kimi,' she said. 'Put down your weapon.'

At first I thought I hadn't heard her correctly. But then I saw her pale hand flash up, and she pointed towards our mother . . .

Mother was on her knees, head tilted back. One of the samurai had twisted his hand into her long black hair and was holding her tightly, exposing her throat to the razor-sharp edge of his long sword.

'No!' I whispered, my heart breaking.

'Put down your weapon, and your mother lives,' Manabu said sharply. 'Do it now.'

I could barely breathe. My gaze was fixed on Mother as I slowly lowered my weapon and placed it on the floor at my feet. One of the samurai darted forward and snatched it up.

'Search her,' Manabu snapped.

The soldier patted me down, checking my kimono for hidden blades. He hesitated when his fingers found the little bamboo *bokken* of Moriyasu's that I wore tucked into my sash. 'Nothing,' he said at last. 'Just a harmless wooden toy.'

Then, with their hands tight on our shoulders, the soldiers forced Hana, Tatsuya, and me down onto our knees at the table.

The samurai still had his hand twisted in Mother's hair.

'Let her go!' I begged. 'I've put down my weapon.'

'I don't think so.' Manabu looked from Mother to Tatsuya and back again, as if he was admiring the sword blades pointed at both their throats. 'I think we might have some fun here instead. How about a little game, eh?'

I stared up at him, confused. 'A game?' I whispered.

'Yes, a game, Kimi-*gozen*,' he sneered at me. 'You were always fond of those. I want you to choose. One person in this room must die . . . ' He shot a hard look at Tatsuya and pressed his blade a little tighter to his throat. 'And Kimi-*gozen* must choose which it will be.'

'Wh-what?' I gaped at him. 'I don't understand.'

'It's really not complicated,' Manabu said. 'Either your friend dies . . . or your mother does.'

I stared up at the manservant in shock, my heart like a cold stone in my chest. 'Wh-why must I choose?'

'I believe that, now, you are the eldest child,' Manabu said with an oily smile. 'And, of course, we must never forget that it is the eldest child who is superior.'

I knew this was an echo of the bitterness Uncle Hidehira felt about Father being chosen as *jito* instead of him.

I stared at Manabu's sallow face and felt a flash of hatred. How could I have been so blind? I had thought this man was our friend. I had trusted him. Only Tatsuya had seen the truth. I flushed with shame and looked at my friend, so noble and dignified despite the sword that glittered at his throat. I thought back to the mud patch on the other side of the lake. Tatsuya must regret saving Manabu's life now.

'I can't choose,' I said hoarsely.

'Oh, but you *will* choose,' Manabu said, his eyes glittering.

Hana shifted restlessly beside me. 'Why are you doing this, Manabu?' she asked in anguish.

'Why do you think I'm doing it?' Manabu said roughly. 'I serve Lord Hidehira, the true *jito.*'

'My father was the true *jito,*' Hana retorted. 'You served him once—or were you pretending even then?'

Manabu's lip curled in a sneer. 'I wouldn't serve Yoshijiro if my life depended on it,' he said. 'That man refused to promote my father.'

My mother's voice came out of the shadows on the far side of the table. 'Your father was a traitor who did not deserve to be promoted,' she said. The samurai had let go of her hair, but the sword still hovered dangerously near her throat.

Manabu ignored her. 'Lord Hidehira, however, recognized talent where he saw it. He promoted my father and made sure I got the best training.' He hammered his fist against his chest. 'He knew how to inspire loyalty!'

Hana was gazing incredulously at Manabu. 'Did

Uncle Hidehira send you to serve Father all those moons ago?' she asked. 'To spy?'

Manabu drew himself up proudly. 'I am samurai!' he exclaimed. 'I serve Lord Hidehira to the death, and I will do anything he asks of me. Yes, he sent me, dressed as a servant, to gather information. I did his bidding gladly, because I knew that one day, when he was in power, his lordship would honour me with land and wealth.'

Hana shook her head. 'So many moons have passed since you came,' she murmured. 'Uncle Hidehira plotted against us all that time.'

I remembered what Manabu had told us about the uprising. How he had rushed to Mother's room to save her and Moriyasu. 'None of the story you told us about the night of the massacre was true, was it?' I said bitterly. 'I bet you were furious when you learned that we had escaped.'

Manabu shrugged. 'I told you part of the story,' he said. 'I did rush to the mistress's room, once Lord Hidehira had begun the killing. But it wasn't to warn her.' He shot Mother a look of venom. 'It was to kill her! The one who brings her to the *jito* will be most rewarded.'

My heart twisted in my chest, and I felt Hana reach sideways to touch my fingertips with her own.

'Too bad she had already run away, like a coward,' Manabu went on, caressing the hilt of his sword as if he would like nothing more than to draw it and finish his mission now, by slicing Mother's head from her shoulders. 'That night I swore to Lord Hidehira that I would track down the woman and her brat. Now I have fulfilled my oath and earned my reward.'

'And we helped you,' Hana said bitterly. 'Tatsuya tried to warn us, but we wouldn't listen.'

'It was so easy to fool you,' Manabu said with a snigger. 'You and your sister . . . rushing up to me at the temple just because you recognized an old friend. I've never seen such foolish girls.'

'How did you get the letter?' I asked.

'Lord Hidehira sent me to the temple,' Manabu replied. 'We hoped we would catch her, but she had delivered the scroll to one of the monks much earlier in the day. I showed the monk my orders from the *jito* and he simply handed over the scroll.' His narrow eyes gleamed. 'With a little help from the point of my sword, of course.'

'You killed a monk?' Mother cried in disbelief.

Manabu shrugged. 'It wouldn't be the first time.' He gave a brisk, mocking bow to me. 'I ought to thank you, really. You led me straight to my target. Without you, I would never have

found them. But as it is . . . well, I have all of you.
A nice family reunion. My lord will be most
appreciative.'

I clenched my fists. How could I have been so
stupid? I cast a look at Mother and Moriyasu.
Mother had her eyes closed. Beside her, my
little brother sat bravely, his face deathly pale
but his eyes blazing with defiance, as if he was
willing himself not to cry. He looked different
somehow—he had grown in the time we had
been apart.

I tried to smile at him. But he simply stared
back at me, his expression unreadable. I bit my lip,
wondering how to get through to him—then at
last I remembered. His little wooden *bokken*! I'd
carried it all this way, through the passing of many
moons, praying that I would have a chance to give
it back to him when we were reunited.

My heart felt lighter as I eased the *bokken* out of
my sash and slid it across the table towards my little brother. His face lit up.

But all at once Manabu leaned over and
sent the *bokken* spinning across the table. 'You are
past the age for toys, Kimi-*gozen*,' he said. 'You
must choose, remember?' He twitched his blade
against Tatsuya's throat. The silvery steel length
glittered, picking up the orange light cast by the

smouldering charcoal brazier in the corner. 'Your friend . . . or your mother.'

The samurai standing behind Mother was tense and ready. Mother opened her eyes and gazed across the table at me. Her face was pale, but her expression was brave and dignified.

I exchanged a horrified glance with Hana.

'Don't look at your sister,' Manabu snarled at me. 'You make this decision alone.'

Sickened, I stared down at the table top. My mother or my friend. How could I choose? How could *anyone* make such a choice? How I wished that Master Goku was there to guide me with his wisdom. What would he say? *Empty your mind, Kimi. Let all your fears slip away until only the truth remains . . .*

But what was the truth?

Surely I had to choose Mother.

But then Tatsuya must die, and that was wrong. He had been a loyal and true friend.

I looked from my mother back to Tatsuya. Could I condemn anyone to death? It was an impossible choice. I had to find a way out of this.

My heart ached. Then Master Goku's voice seemed to rise within me, soft and gentle as a summer breeze. *Empty your mind, Kimi. Let all your fears slip away . . .*

And from nowhere, the truth came to me.

There might be a way I could save both Mother *and* Tatsuya. Back at the *dojo*, Uncle Hidehira had ordered that my mother and brother should be brought back to him alive. Manabu wouldn't dare go against the wishes of the *jito*, so that meant he was relying on me choosing Mother, leaving him free to kill Tatsuya. I knew he meant to kill us all eventually, but Manabu would have to delay killing Mother—and the possibility was enough for me to take the risk. The blood began to pulse through my veins, hard and fast.

I looked across the table, straight into my mother's dark eyes, willing her to understand.

'I choose Tatsuya,' I said.

chapter 16

Beside me, Hana gasped in shock. Tatsuya jumped as if a jellyfish had stung him.

Manabu's eyebrows shot up in surprise, but he gave a curt nod. 'So be it,' he said. 'You have made your choice.'

My mother's face turned as pale as ash. As she turned her head away, the hurt expression in her eyes twisted a knife in my heart. But there was no time to explain because at a signal from Manabu, the samurai behind Mother twisted his hand once more into her hair and dragged her to her feet.

Manabu turned to me. 'I will take her and the boy outside and kill them now,' he snapped. 'As for you, my samurai will dispatch you.'

I tried to scramble to my feet, but Manabu shoved me back down onto my knees with a snarl. 'Bring back their heads,' he said to his men.

Behind him, I saw Moriyasu snatch up his little *bokken* from the table and swing it at Manabu's back . . .

But he didn't land a blow. One of the samurai, a wiry man with the eyes of a dead fish, snatched up my brother. He slung him easily over one shoulder and marched out of the hut. The last I saw of Moriyasu was his desperate little face.

'Kimi,' he whispered and the sound broke my heart again. His eyes pleaded with me. But there was nothing I could do.

My mother stared at me in confusion as she left in the guard of two samurai.

As I watched them go, Hana caught my hand. Her fingers were icy cold. Tatsuya was staring at the doorway, looking numb.

The bamboo screen door closed with a snap. I heard Manabu give a curt order outside, although his words were muffled and I couldn't make out what he said. Was he giving orders to kill Mother and Moriyasu? Perhaps my plan was about to go tragically wrong . . .

Moments later the sound of horses' hooves echoed through the hut. I prayed that Manabu was following his orders from the *jito*. Surely the fact that they were leaving meant that he was taking Mother and Moriyasu back to Uncle Hidehira, and not killing them as he had threatened.

The three guards who remained in the hut with us were drawing their swords.

One of the samurai gave an evil grin. 'Boy,' he said to Tatsuya, 'leave now, or die with them.'

I looked at Tatsuya, who was staring at me with a stunned expression. Finally, he blinked, his face adopting a mask of defiance as he eyed the samurai. 'She chose to save my life,' he said, adopting a guard stance with his bladeless hands. 'Now I choose to help preserve hers . . .'

The samurai raised his sword. 'Then all three of you shall die.'

'Not today,' I muttered through gritted teeth.

I held on tight to Hana's hand and leapt to my feet, pulling her up with me. Tatsuya was beside me as we slipped around the table. I tried to keep the rough-hewn wood between us and the heavily-armed soldiers.

I caught Hana glancing at me. Her eyes were full of anger and I knew she blamed me for what might happen to Mother and Moriyasu.

'I didn't betray them,' I tried to tell her, but my words died in my throat as one of the samurai lunged across the table in an attempt to run me through.

I leaped backwards, and the sword whispered as it sliced the empty air.

The samurai with no helmet edged around the table to engage with Tatsuya.

'Manabu won't kill Mother and Moriyasu,' I told Hana breathlessly as the other two men bore down on us. They trod stealthily, like cats stalking mice. 'Uncle Hidehira wants them brought to him alive, remember?'

An expression of confusion flickered across Hana's face, and I knew I had to make her understand.

'It's more than Manabu's life is worth to kill Mother,' I said, desperately avoiding another whistling blade. 'That's why I chose Tatsuya . . . '

'You shouldn't have,' Tatsuya cut in. He ducked away from a samurai who aimed a blow at his head. 'I'm grateful, Kimi. But it wasn't worth the risk.' His jaw tightened.

'We can rescue Mother and Moriyasu!' I cried desperately to Hana, just as Tatsuya flung up a wooden bowl and caught the edge of the samurai's blade with it.

Tatsuya's arms jarred with the impact, and then suddenly he was staggering. I was shocked to see that he held two pieces of bowl in his hands. The bowl was cut as cleanly as if it had been made of wax.

The samurai brought his sword back up with a grunt, but Tatsuya leapt away from him, up onto the table. He reached up high and managed to grab an iron lantern bracket, wrenched it hard, and tore it free from its fixings.

I kept my gaze fixed on my own opponent, and we circled each other warily.

Beside me, Hana dived at the samurai nearest to her, surprising him by throwing her arms around his waist as if she was dancing. The next moment, I saw her hand flash at his waist. She had grabbed his knife!

With a wild yell, Tatsuya wielded the iron lantern bracket like a sword. He brought it down on the bare head of the samurai who was attacking him. I heard a bone-crunching thud, and the samurai's eyes rolled up in his head. He pitched forward, lifeless as a rag doll.

Hana held the knife she had snatched, her eyes searching for a gap in her opponent's armour. Still circling my opponent, I cast around desperately for a weapon of my own . . . but there was nothing. The only furnishings were the heavy table, a few straw mats, and the charcoal brazier.

The brazier! With a yell of triumph, I leapt backwards, caught the edge of the brazier with my foot and flipped it up, dashing it into the face of my opponent.

Hot, bright coals sprayed out.

The samurai shrieked in agony, and clawed at his burning face.

I flipped the brazier again and sent another shower of coals and sparks at the third samurai. He screamed and turned blindly towards the door. Tatsuya gave him a hard shove and he smashed straight through the bamboo screen, staggered momentarily, and then disappeared at a run.

A moment of stunned silence was broken by a groan from the samurai with the burned face. I turned to look at him and saw that he was on his knees, his blackened head cupped in his hands. I knew that even if he recovered from his wounds he would probably never fight again.

Hana was staring at him, her expression one of sickened shock.

I seized my sister by the hands, turning her to face me. 'Hana, look at me!' When I had her attention, I went on, 'Everything's going to be all right. We'll rescue Mother and Moriyasu.'

Behind us, Tatsuya began to gather up our weapons.

Hana's gaze was still fixed on me. 'I'm glad you saved Tatsuya's life, Kimi,' she said in a quiet and somehow desolate voice. 'But how can we rescue them? We don't even know where Manabu is taking them.'

'Yes, we do,' I insisted. 'He'll take them to Uncle Hidehira. And Uncle Hidehira will be with the army in the east. They're preparing to strike at the *jito*'s stronghold in Sagami.'

Tatsuya was crouching down by the wounded samurai. He looked up at me in amazement. 'How do you know that?' he asked.

'The captain at the inn told us,' I reminded him. 'He said that if we wanted to fight Lord Hidehira then we should head east, to Sagami.'

'So he did.' Tatsuya straightened up.

'But Manabu and his men have horses,' Hana said hesitantly, an expression of hope beginning to dawn across her face. 'We can't hope to catch them . . .'

'Not on foot,' I agreed. 'But there's the river. It flows fast, away to the east.'

Tatsuya nodded. 'We'll need that boat again,' he said. 'Let's get out of here.'

Together, we hurried out of the hut and made our way along the main street. The little town was still deserted. The boat was still lashed to a wooden post sticking up out of the water, but the fisherman was nowhere in sight.

'Should we try to find him?' Hana asked, looking around anxiously.

'That would take too long,' I said. 'We have to catch up with Manabu.'

I clenched my fist, thinking hard, then came to a decision. 'I think we should take the boat,' I said.

Tatsuya and Hana looked at me in astonishment.

'You mean, steal it?' Hana asked.

I shook my head. 'It's not stealing if we pay for it,' I pointed out, and fished the innkeeper's leather money bag out of my kimono. 'We need this boat. We *can't* let Manabu take Mother and Moriyasu to Uncle,' I said. 'If the fisherman knew the truth, I'm sure he'd understand.'

Quickly I looped the money bag over the top of the wooden post. 'He'll find the money when he comes for his boat,' I said. 'There should be more than enough in there to pay for a replacement— and maybe some food for his family.'

'But we don't know how to scull,' Hana said.

'I do,' Tatsuya said. 'And you two can help using those poles.' Tatsuya indicated two long pieces of wood secured to one side of the boat.

We settled ourselves in the boat, untied the

rope from the wooden post, and pushed away from the shore. Tatsuya began to manoeuvre the little boat and I half expected to hear a shout, but the village remained deserted as we glided past. Somewhere a dog barked, but otherwise we slid along the river in silence.

We soon left the town behind. The sun was rising higher in the sky, sparkling off the surface of the water. I guessed it must be mid-morning, although I couldn't be sure. A current picked us up, bearing us quickly down-river.

It felt strange to be journeying again. I had been so focused on the reunion with Mother and Moriyasu, the end of our journey—and how fleeting that reunion had turned out to be. I bit my lip and gazed at the swirling green river. Had I made the right decision? What if I was wrong and we couldn't rescue them?

'Watch those rocks!' Hana's voice broke into my thoughts.

Black boulders rose from the water on either side of the boat, looking like teeth in the jaws of an enormous dragon. We used the long poles to steer away from them, and headed ever eastwards towards the border. Occasionally we passed places where huts and hovels clustered on the riverbank. There were fruit orchards, rice fields, and willow trees that dipped their branches in the cool, clear water.

A couple of times, Tatsuya stared across the river and into the trees, his dark eyes alert.

'What are you looking for?' I asked.

Tatsuya hesitated, and then dragged his gaze away from the riverbank to look at me for a moment. 'Nothing,' he said. 'I was just watching out for signs that we might be nearing the border with Sagami.'

The sun moved across the sky as we glided on. Tatsuya began to explain how he steered the boat and Hana and I each had a turn.

After some time, the scenery changed to denser forests.

'I think we must be quite near the border,' I said, glancing back over my shoulder to where Mount Fuji rose up far in the distance. I frowned, trying to remember what I had seen on the scrolls from my father's study at home. 'I think the river curves and there are lots of rocks just before Kai Province becomes Sagami.'

Hana was staring ahead along the river, her hand tight on the side of the boat. 'I can see plenty of rocks just at the next bend,' she said. 'The water is rougher there, too.'

Tatsuya took over the sculling, his gaze fixed on

the bend in the river as we approached. Rocks reared up on either side of us, slick and wet. Tatsuya began to struggle to keep control of the boat on the swells. The river around us started to churn.

'We're entering rapids,' Tatsuya said, looking anxious as I was forced to use the pole to push us away from a rock that loomed close.

'Look!' Hana cried, pointing to the shore as she clung to the side of the boat. 'There's a marker. Do you think that shows where Kai Province crosses into Sagami?'

I turned to look, and saw an enormous pole sticking out of the riverbank. Carved and lacquered with green and gold, it seemed to glow in the mid-morning sunshine. I could just make out a tumble of black painted *kanji* characters running from the top down.

'Sagami Province . . .' I said breathlessly.

'Is that a person on the other side of the marker?' Hana was staring into the trees.

Was there? I narrowed my eyes, but saw only a shadow cast by a willow tree, and then there was no time to wonder because Tatsuya was calling for our assistance. I braced myself and kept the long pole at the ready. The boat tipped and tilted, taking on water, and Hana went down on her knees to bail, sloshing water over the side with her cupped hands.

Pitching and tossing, our little boat swept through the last of the rocks. Then suddenly, it came to rest in a wide stretch of river where the water was as calm and tranquil as a lily pond on a summer's day.

'That was more difficult than I expected,' I said breathlessly. 'But we made it!'

'How far should we travel on the river?' Hana asked uncertainly.

Tatsuya squinted up at the sky. 'I think we should go on until the sun reaches its highest point,' he said. 'Then we'll moor, and head inland towards the south.'

I nodded. 'That should take us close to the town where Uncle will be preparing for his attack.'

Hana was still looking around, a tiny frown creasing her brow. 'Something's not right,' she said in a low voice. 'I can feel danger close by.'

I followed her gaze, watching the way the willow trees swept over the riverbank to dapple the calm water. 'I can't see anything out of the ordinary,' I murmured.

I turned to look at Tatsuya, my eyebrows raised. He looked tense and watchful.

In the water behind him, a fish leaped. Silver

ripples widened across the surface of the green water. I smiled and began to turn away. But all at once, the surface rippled again and broke apart in three places. Black forms rose up from the river.

The world seemed to move in slow motion. I caught my breath as the forms solidified in front of my horrified gaze. Heads, necks, shoulders, and arms. Masked men dressed entirely in black. Dark eyes glittered like black ice from the narrow slits cut in their masks. Steel blades flashed between their fingers.

Ninja!

chapter 17

Standing waist deep in the water, one of the ninja grabbed Tatsuya.

My sword already in my hand, I leaped to my feet. 'Let him go!' I yelled. But my sudden movement made the boat lurch dangerously. I was aware of Hana shouting, arms flailing, and then she vanished over the side of the boat as I fell to my knees.

A hand came around me from behind, clamping tightly across my mouth to stifle my cry. My sword was snatched away from me. Powerful fingers closed around my throat, moving quickly. There was a brief sensation of pressure on either side of my neck—and abruptly all the energy I possessed drained away.

I couldn't move!

All I could do was blink in astonishment. Who *were* these people? To disarm a person and stun them just with a touch!

I could not move my arms and legs.

I could see clearly, though. Across the boat, Tatsuya was fighting desperately, hands clawed against a ninja's black-masked face. But he was no match. The ninja disabled him, fingers twisting lightly against Tatsuya's chest—and suddenly Tatsuya was still.

'Cowards,' he managed to say, the cords in his neck standing out with the effort to speak. 'I won't let you take me! I won't!'

Hana came surging up out of the water on the far side of the boat. She swung her *nihonto* sword wide, and I felt a swell of hope.

But in the next instant the third man was at her side. He snatched her sword and pushed her hard so that she lost her balance and fell backwards again with an enormous splash. I tried to force myself to move . . . to reach her . . . but I was still under the influence of whatever strange hold the ninja had put over my energies.

The three black shapes converged on Tatsuya. I

caught a brief glimpse of his desperate expression, and then the ninja climbed out of the river as silently as they had come, taking Tatsuya with them. When they reached dry land, he kicked out, once, and then was still as they bore him away into the trees that lined the river.

Hana had been under water so long, I thought for a moment that she had drowned, but at last her dark head broke the surface. She came up quickly, gasping for air. When she saw me, standing motionless, she waded through the water to my side.

'Oh, Kimi!' she exclaimed. 'What have they done to you?'

'I can't move,' I managed to say, half sobbing. 'Help me!'

'Don't panic.' Hana put her hands on my arms, her face soothing. 'I think I can fix this. Harumasa once asked me to copy a set of scrolls about pressure points and how they might be used in a fight.' She frowned, placing a careful forefinger against my throat. 'I never imagined I would one day have to use the knowledge on my own sister.'

I felt her cool touch against my skin, like the kiss of a rose petal. She pressed, and then twisted the tip of her thumb against me. A sensation of lightness and freedom flooded through my limbs.

Amazed, I opened and closed the fingers of my left hand, and then my right. I could move again!

'Thank you, Hana.' I hugged her quickly and then turned to stare at the riverbank, studying the spot where the ninja had disappeared. 'We have to go after them!'

But Hana shook her head. 'We can never hope to find them, Kimi,' she said quietly. 'If the ninja have taken Tatsuya, then it is for a reason. They won't let us take him back. And they have all our weapons, so we're no match for them now.'

I turned to stare at her. 'Are you saying we have to leave Tatsuya to whatever fate the ninja have in store for him?'

'Yes,' Hana said simply. Her eyes were wide and clear as she held my gaze. 'You chose Tatsuya once, Kimi. You can't choose him again. We have to go after Mother and Moriyasu now.'

I clenched my fists. 'But we can't just abandon him!' I cried. 'He's our friend. He helped us when nobody else would . . . ' I thought of the way he had stood up to Uncle Hidehira in the *dojo* temple, and the way he had fought so bravely in the glade.

'I don't want to leave him any more than you do. Tatsuya is special.' Hana turned away and heaved herself back into the boat. She picked up the oar and looked at me. 'But we have no choice, Kimi,' she said. 'If we don't reach the stronghold, Mother and Moriyasu will be executed, and all hope will be lost.'

I knew she was right. And although it hurt me to turn my back on Tatsuya, I mastered my emotion and climbed into the boat beside my sister.

'I don't know how you can give Tatsuya up so easily,' I muttered. 'He's our friend.'

'Mother needs us more,' Hana said, her eyes flashing as she grabbed the steering oar. 'Now are you going to help me row this boat, or not?'

I clenched my jaw, angry with her—angry with everything that had been happening—then snatched up one of the long poles and thrust it deep into the water.

We sculled in silence, awkward with each other for the first time in our lives. Hana and I had never argued before. There had never been anything to argue about.

The sun moved slowly towards the highest point in the sky, following its age-old pattern. Our clothes soon dried. But despite the warmth of the sun I felt cold inside, as if a shard of ice had lodged somewhere beneath my heart. I couldn't help feeling that we had let down Tatsuya when he had needed us most. Questions jostled through my mind. What would become of him? Why did the ninja want him?

I swallowed hard, bitterly regretting the way I had teased Tatsuya about being jumpy about the ninja bush. It seemed he had had good reason to be nervous. And now they had taken him, just as they had taken his father so many years ago.

Hana's gentle voice broke into my thoughts. 'Do you think we've gone far enough, Kimi?' she asked. 'We must be well inside the borders of Sagami Province now. Tatsuya said we should carry on until the sun reached its highest point, then head inland.'

I glanced at her. Her dark gaze held mine and I saw that she was trying to make peace between us as best she could.

I shifted my stick and leaned forward to touch her hand. 'You're right,' I said. 'We should do as Tatsuya said. Head inland towards the south, and find Lord Kanahara's stronghold.'

We spotted a good landing place where the riverbank dipped down towards the water. There was a grove of trees nearby, the fresh green leaves rustling in the wind. I rolled up the bottoms of my *hakama* trousers and went over the side, dragging the boat behind me as I waded ashore.

Hana climbed out and together we tied the boat to a slender sapling.

'There,' I said. 'We'll leave it there for whoever wants it.'

'It will be a lucky find for someone,' Hana said with a smile.

Friends again, we turned to walk away together, intending to strike out for the south.

Instead, we found ourselves face to face with six drawn swords.

chapter 18

A group of boys, older than we were, held their gleaming steel blades high, ready to fight. They wore colourful, patterned kimono jackets in reds and bright oranges, and green *hakama* trousers which had been knotted at the knee.

'By the style of your clothes, I'd guess you've come from Kai Province,' said the tallest boy. He had unusual light-green eyes. His jet-black hair had been roughly cut to just above his shoulders, the top portion twisted up into a leather lace on the back of his head.

'And by the style of *your* clothes, I'd guess you're Sagami born and bred,' I retorted.

'Then you'd guess right,' the green-eyed boy said with a curt nod. 'Which makes me someone who's walking on home territory, whilst you are trespassing. What are you doing here?'

One of the others had been staring at Hana. 'I know what they're doing here, Yorio,' he said to his leader. He was a short, thick-set boy who had the sort of face that looked as if it was ready to break into a grin at a moment's notice. He wasn't grinning now, though. He looked serious and guarded, and his long sword was held ready. 'Their Lord Hidehira is so desperate to steal our land that he's even sending girls to fight,' he said, still staring at Hana.

I glanced at my sister and silently cursed that I had not reminded her to tie her hair back up after the struggle with the ninjas. She had left it loose to dry it after her tumble into the river.

'I may be a girl,' Hana said, meeting the thick-set boy's gaze calmly, 'but I can fight as well as any boy.'

'That sounds like a challenge to me, Norio!' cried one of the other boys.

Norio shifted his centre of gravity, weighing his sword in his hand as he eyed Hana. 'You want to test your theory?' he asked, eyebrows raised. 'Or are you afraid to fight?'

'I'm not afraid to fight anyone,' Hana said firmly.

'We're not here to do battle with you,' I interrupted, staring at Yorio, the leader.

'No?' He stared back at me, his green eyes glittering dangerously. 'Well that's too bad, because we are. We're here scouting along the river to make sure that none of the enemy sneaks across the border from Kai Province. Everyone in Sagami has sworn to resist your new *jito* and anyone he sends to spy on us.'

'We're not spies!' Hana protested.

But she got no further, because Norio moved in.

He struck quickly, and there was nothing Hana could do except duck away and try to evade his singing blade. I leaped in front of her, but Yorio blocked me. We circled warily for a moment, each of us measuring the other.

From the corner of my eye, I saw Hana snatch up a branch from the ground. She swung it at Norio and he deflected with the flat of his blade. I could not worry about my sister, though, because Yorio came dancing towards me with his long sword in his hand. He was so close I could see the tiny leaf pattern embroidered into his kimono.

'Let's see what kind of fighters you boys from Kai Province really are,' he said in a mocking lilt. Swiftly, he lunged forward, but not with his sword. He swiped at me with his fist.

I narrowed my eyes, my mind racing as I twisted away. What was he doing? Although his sword was in his hand, he made no move to use it. I centred myself, hands out in front of me, watching his every move.

'Come on,' Yorio taunted as he lunged again.

Hana and Norio were locked in combat, his blade striking against her branch with hollow clashes. As Yorio and I danced back and forth, cat and mouse, the band of boys moved to surround us. Some of them shouted encouragement to their leader. My heart began to pound. My breathing was taut and shallow. Yorio came in again. His sword was still held wide, ready to fight, but he made no attempt to use his blade.

I ducked away, all the while trying desperately to read him. I had never seen someone fight like this. What was he doing?

Yorio feinted left with his upper body and then stepped immediately to the right. Confused, I faltered. And in that moment of confusion, he had me. His foot flashed sideways, catching my ankles, lifting, hooking . . .

All at once I was flat on my back, the breath knocked from my body.

The boys around us cheered triumphantly. One of them punched a fist in the air, his bright orange sleeve rippling.

I cursed myself silently. I knew that this defeat was my own fault. Both my teachers, Master Goku and Father, would have told me that I had thought too much during the fight. I had spent too much time wondering about my opponent and his intention.

Now I would pay the price.

Yorio's steel sword flashed as he lightly placed the tip against my throat. 'Yield,' he said, his green eyes fixed on mine. There was no pressure behind his blade, but the threat was there. Behind him, Hana and Norio were suddenly still.

'I yield,' I said in a respectful tone, holding Yorio's gaze. 'But you should know that I am not your enemy. And nor are you mine.'

Yorio frowned. 'What is this?' he asked. 'A riddle?'

'It's no riddle,' I said. 'We are both engaged in the same fight—*against* Lord Hidehira.'

'It's true,' Hana said. 'We're not spies . . . ' I could see her weighing things up in her mind. She glanced at me, took a deep breath, and blurted out, 'We're not spies—we're rebels.'

There was a moment of silence. Nothing seemed to move on the riverbank. Yorio held me with his gaze, his blade still tight to my throat. Behind him, Norio and a couple of the other boys exchanged glances.

Then at last Yorio seemed to make a decision. He took his blade from my throat and nodded at me. 'Stand up,' he said.

I scrambled to my feet, noticing that he didn't sheath his sword but held it ready. He was watching me warily. 'Tell me why you're here,' he commanded. 'Hidehira is your Lord Steward and you are sworn to serve him . . .'

I shook my head. 'Not us,' I said. 'We refuse to swear allegiance to that murderer. He killed our father and older brothers . . . burnt our home . . . turned our friends against us.' I swallowed hard because the words felt thick in my throat. 'And we will have our revenge for that.'

Yorio's eyes narrowed. 'That's quite a story,' he said. 'How do I know it's true?'

'You'll have to take my word for it,' I said simply.

He looked me up and down, scrutinizing my clothing. 'Let's say I believe you,' he said at last.

'Answer me this—where are you going, and why are you travelling without weapons?'

'We had weapons but they were stolen when we were attacked up river,' I said, and quickly told him about the ninja in the water. He was surprised to hear of ninja lurking on the estates and sent one of the boys to inform the scouts to keep a lookout.

'And as to where we're heading,' I went on, 'we're not sure, but we know it's a town nearby, your *jito*'s stronghold. Hidehira is gathering an army close by and preparing to attack.'

Yorio exchanged a quick glance with Norio. 'We know this already,' he said. 'Our own spies have been scouting the countryside, bringing back word of where his soldiers are gathering.' He fell silent for a moment, looking thoughtful. A light breeze stirred the trees along the riverbank and out in the water a fish leaped, silver-bright.

At last, Yorio seemed to reach a decision. 'You both fight well,' he said. 'We need fighters like you if we are to defeat Lord Hidehira and restore peace to our land. You say that you are heading to our *jito*'s stronghold, to fight against Hidehira. Well, we have a common aim—because tonight we also march to the *jito*'s stronghold. We intend to surprise the armies massed outside the town walls. There are only two of you, whereas at our *dojo* there are hundreds gathering to fight shoulder to shoulder against the *Kaminari*.' He caught my gaze and held it. 'What if I asked you to join us?'

Hana and I stared at each other, astounded. We both knew that this would be our best chance of rescuing Mother and Moriyasu. Hana gave a tiny nod, and my heart leaped with hope and excitement.

I turned to Yorio and bowed respectfully. 'We would be honoured,' I said.

The boys all sheathed their weapons. 'This way,' said Yorio, and led us all away from the riverbank.

Norio fell into step with Hana. 'You fight very well,' he said, his voice full of admiration.

'Thank you,' Hana said, hiding her smile behind her hand. 'I suppose you mean I fight well for a girl.'

Norio laughed. 'I used to spar with my sister sometimes,' he said. 'But she wasn't as fast on her feet as you are.'

Yorio slowed his pace and let his stride match mine as we made our way along a wide path that led through a grove of leafy trees. 'Have you had any formal training?' he asked.

'Hana and I both studied under Master Goku for some time.'

'Master Goku is a legend,' he said, eyebrows raised. 'We've all heard stories about him, many times. The master of our *dojo* is a great friend of his. Master Jin—you may have heard of him?'

I nodded. I recognized his name as one that Goku used to correspond with regularly, although it had been interrupted by Lord Hidehira's recent declaration of hostility towards Lord Kanahara.

'I didn't know they allowed girls to train at the *dojo*,' Norio said.

Hana smiled. 'They don't,' she said. 'He didn't know we were girls when we first arrived there. That came later.'

Norio looked confused. 'What do you mean?' he asked.

I turned to glance at him over my shoulder. 'We both disguised ourselves as boys and presented ourselves at the *dojo* for training,' I said.

Norio gaped. 'You mean . . . you mean . . . y-you're a girl too?' he stuttered.

Grinning, I reached up for the pin that secured my top-knot and tugged it loose so that my long hair tumbled down over my shoulders.

There was a gasp from one of the boys. 'He's a girl!' someone cried.

Abruptly Yorio started to laugh. 'What's your name?' he asked.

'Kimi,' I said, combing my hair with my fingers. 'My name's Kimi.' I felt a rush of pleasure at telling someone my real name for the first time in many moon phases.

We had left the river far behind us now and were walking south, heading uphill through a wood where monkeys chattered and shrieked. Dust and pollen danced in the shafts of afternoon sunlight that slanted down through the trees. The pathway forked and twisted, reached the crest of the hill, and eventually began to run alongside a high wall.

'Behind this wall is the *dojo* compound,' Yorio explained, as we all made our way towards an enormous gate set into the wall. 'We have many courtyards and gardens, and the largest practice hall in Sagami!'

The gates were thick and imposing with wooden spikes sticking out at the top. Two armed men in steel helmets stood guard outside, but they bowed low when they saw Yorio and hurried to swing open a small door set into the gate.

I glanced around with interest as we stepped over the threshold. The compound was very much like Master Goku's *dojo*. Big square courtyards, the sand neatly raked, sweeping maple trees, and glimpses of wooden walkways which led through moss gardens. Away to the left I could see a cluster of students in dove-grey kimonos standing on a narrow bridge over a lily pond, and beyond them the flash of steel as someone engaged in practice combat.

'Welcome to our *dojo*,' Yorio said with a low bow. 'I will take you immediately to Master Jin.' He turned to his friends, 'You go and prepare for the assault.'

Norio and the other boys said goodbye and left us, making their way purposefully towards a long, low building with a wood shingle rooftop which I took to be the practice hall.

Hana and I followed Yorio along a series of neat gravel pathways. We passed a knot of students who all straightened their shoulders as Yorio approached, and bowed respectfully as we passed.

'Have you studied here for a long time?' I asked.

'All my life,' he replied with a smile. 'Master Jin is my father.'

'Oh!' I was impressed. Perhaps this explained why Yorio had such unusual fighting techniques. Master Jin must have been training his son since he had learned to walk.

We passed a garden where a group of students sat quietly in meditation. We went up a flight of stone steps and found ourselves on a wide terrace that looked out over the hillside. Yorio indicated that we should wait, and then hurried away, disappearing through an archway at the far end of the terrace.

Hana and I made our way to the wooden balustrade at the edge of the terrace and stared out at the view.

I realized at once how high we had climbed to reach the training school. The river where we had left our boat was now far below, a slender ribbon of blue cutting through the wide valley. Green woodland hatched the hillside, only partly concealing the clusters of rooftops here and there that signified small villages. I wondered if Tatsuya was out there somewhere, still struggling to get free.

Some distance away, in a haze of coppery late afternoon sunlight, a great compound reared up from inside a hastily built shelter of fences, felled trees, and ditches. The town knew it would soon be besieged, and it had prepared for the battle as best it could. The rooftops of its few watchtowers twisted upwards like the shoulder-guards of samurai armour. On another hillside I could see the curving roof of another *dojo* and beyond that, yet another.

'These estates are full of training schools,' Hana said in wonder.

Behind us, a cool, light voice drifted across the terrace. 'We will need our students to be well-trained, for the fighting that is to come.'

Hana and I turned to see a stern-looking man making his way across the terrace towards us. He was tall and very thin, with high cheekbones. Simple dove-grey robes matched his grey hair. His eyes were the same unusual green as Yorio's.

He came to a halt in front of us and bowed low. 'You must be Hana and Kimi,' he said. 'I am Master Jin.'

243

We both bowed low, bringing our fingers close together across the front of our thighs to show our respect.

Master Jin led us to a long wooden bench set beneath a red maple tree at the far end of the terrace.

'Yorio has told me that you wish to join our fight,' he said, when we were all seated. 'He explained that Hidehira murdered your father and brothers, and that you were forced to dress as boys and take refuge in a samurai training school. In time, I would like to hear more of those events.

But first, will you give me news of my great friend Master Goku? It is some moons now since we corresponded, much to my sadness.'

My heart sank as I realized that news of Master Goku's death had not travelled as far as Sagami. With a small bow, I said, 'My sister and I carry terrible news. Master Goku is dead.'

Master Jin looked shocked, but he controlled his emotions quickly. 'How did this happen?' he asked.

Haltingly, I told him about the fight between Master Goku and Lord Hidehira's son Ken-ichi. Master Jin held my gaze, but when I finished speaking he looked away for a moment. A wave of pain and anger passed across his face. 'Goku was a great man,' he murmured. 'He should not have died in such a way, weakened by poison and defeated by an unworthy opponent!'

He was silent for a moment, and Hana and I folded our hands in our laps, giving him as much time as he needed. But at last he spoke again, 'Will you tell me about the events which have led you here?'

Taking turns to speak, Hana and I told him about our time at the *dojo* and our journey to Mount Fuji. I found myself speaking of my brothers, who had also been students of Master

Goku, as had our father and Uncle Hidehira long ago.

At last I came to a halt. Master Jin folded his hands into his wide sleeves. 'Your father was Lord Yoshijiro,' he said calmly, his words more a statement than a question. 'Are you the only members of the Yamamoto family to have survived the uprising?'

Hana shook her head. 'Our mother and little brother Moriyasu managed to escape as well.' I could see the pain in her eyes as she went on. 'We journeyed far to find them, but they were taken again. We think she and Moriyasu are being taken to where the armies are gathering outside your *jito*'s stronghold. That's why we want to go with your soldiers—somehow we must get into the camp and rescue them before Uncle Hidehira puts them to death!'

Master Jin raised his hand. 'And so you shall,' he said. 'Moriyasu must be saved, because he is the rightful heir to the stewardship. He is the true *jito*, and under his young rule the land will be restored to order and there will be peace between our Provinces, as there was when your father was steward.'

Hana and I had carried our burden alone for so long that I felt suddenly weak with relief to know that someone was on our side. Master Jin understood. He was willing to help us. We all had the same goal—to defeat Uncle Hidehira and restore honour to my family.

Master Jin stood up in a ripple of grey robes and went to stand at the balustrade. As he moved I realized there was something about him that reminded me of Goku. Although both men were very different in looks, they had the same inner serenity and wise, calm manner.

Master Jin beckoned Hana and me to the balustrade. 'That is our *jito*'s stronghold,' he told us, pointing towards the *shinden* complex surrounded by a stone wall in the distance. 'My scouts tell me that even now, Hidehira's army is massing just outside the makeshift barriers, preparing their attack as they await the arrival of their lord. If Hidehira takes the town, then the rest of these estates will surely fall, and we will be plunged into chaos.'

I tried to remember Uncle's words to Mister Choji in the tea pavilion, the morning of Goku's funeral. 'I fear my uncle plans to seize the whole Kingdom of Japan in his grasp,' I said.

Master Jin turned and regarded me for a moment. 'I know,' he said sadly. 'It would have broken Master Goku's heart to see such a thing.'

I clenched my fist. 'Hidehira must be stopped,' I said.

'And he will be,' Master Jin said. 'Walk with me, Kimi and Hana.' He gestured the way with his hand. 'I have something I wish to show you.'

As we made our way across the terrace and through a wooden archway, Master Jin talked. 'For many moons, we have had free trade with your estates. Lord Yoshijiro treated neighbouring provinces with respect. There has been peace between our people for almost a generation. Hidehira may think he has power, but there is more to being a lord than grinding everyone beneath your heels. Your father understood that.'

We walked beneath the wooden archway and came to a walkway which led over a lily pond towards an enormous inner courtyard shaded by trees. A hundred or so students were gathered there. Some of them were testing weapons, holding blades up to the light or weighing spears in their hands. Others knelt on mats, sleeves rolled back as they rubbed oil into hardened leather armour. A couple of servants hurried back and forth, handing out iron helmets and *o-sode* shoulder guards. The scene reminded me of the morning of the Great Tournament, when we had all prepared for combat.

'As Yorio has told you,' Master Jin said, 'we are planning a surprise attack on Hidehira's troops tonight. He has focused all his attention on the *jito*'s *shinden*—but he has forgotten that there are many samurai training schools situated in the hills outside the town.'

'How many training schools?' Hana asked.

'Four,' Master Jin said. 'And all of us have been plotting with local villagers to ambush Hidehira's troops before they can make the first strike on the barriers.'

'When is Hidehira's first strike planned?' I asked.

'Our scouts say tomorrow,' Master Jin said gravely. 'They will attack the stronghold at first light.'

'And you will stop them.' Watching the activity in the main courtyard, I felt a thrill of hope and anticipation. I turned to Master Jin, my heart singing. 'We will fight alongside your students,' I said firmly. 'And during the attack we will search for Mother and Moriyasu.'

Master Jin bowed. 'It is imperative that young Master Moriyasu is rescued, if these lands are ever to be at peace again. Our attack on Hidehira's troops will be a distraction. Guards will be drawn away, allowing you and your sister to search. Your goal must be to free them.'

I turned to Hana. 'What do you think?' I asked.

She nodded, her dark eyes shining like black pearls. 'I think that karma led us here,' she said. 'We have more chance of success with Master Jin than we would ever have had on our own.'

Master Jin gestured to Yorio, who was standing nearby. 'Ask one of the servants to fetch Kimi and Hana some food,' he said. 'And then make sure they are armed. They are coming with us tonight!'

chapter 19

usk came early that evening, settling across the land like a velvet cloak. Four stars glinted in the sky far above as Hana and I knelt side by side on a mat at the edge of the courtyard. I gazed upward, thinking about Tatsuya. I wondered where his captors had taken him and offered a small prayer that he was safe and unharmed.

Hana gently touched my hand, gazing up at the sky. 'Those four stars signify you and me, Mother and Moriyasu,' she said. 'After tonight, we'll be together again.'

'I hope so,' I said.

'Surely you know, Kimi.' Hana turned to

meet my gaze, her face questioning. 'Don't you?'

Thoughtfully, I smoothed my thumb over the lacquered hilt of my new sword. The blade was long and curved, beautifully forged, and the scabbard had an engraving of a dragon chasing a flame. When I tested the weight, it felt alive in my hand. Yorio had made sure we had armour, daggers, swords, and short spears. Hana had even found a *nihonto* that was as perfectly balanced as the one the ninja had taken from her.

I sighed and turned back to Hana. 'No, I *don't* know,' I said. 'Even if we survive, who is to say that we will save Mother and Moriyasu? For all we know, they may already be dead.'

Hana looked down at her lap. 'I would have felt it if Uncle had already killed them,' she murmured. 'They're still alive, Kimi. I know they are.'

'I pray that you are right,' I said. 'But we must be realistic about our chances. This could be the last night of their lives . . . and of ours.'

Hana nodded soberly. 'This is the first time we've ever gone to a fight knowing that,' she said. 'It's a strange feeling.'

'Father always said not to fear death, but to embrace it,' I said. 'He told his men to walk with death at their shoulder, shadowing their every footstep.'

Hana nodded. 'If we accept death,' she said. 'Then fear of it cannot be used as a weapon against us.'

As dusk deepened in the sky above, the courtyard seemed to hum with energy. More students came, packing the gravel square. I saw villagers join them, armed with sickles from the rice fields.

I spotted Yorio threading his way through the crowd towards us. He had a small bowl cupped in his hands.

'Smear some of this mud on your faces,' he said. 'It will help to keep you hidden.'

We dipped our fingers into the cool mud and pasted it across our cheeks.

Yorio crouched in front of Hana and me, and told us the plan for tonight's surprise attack. 'Stay with me,' he instructed. 'Everyone from the *dojo* is going to make their way down the hill into the valley. The scouts have arranged a time for simultaneous strike attack from all sides under cover of darkness.' Yorio grinned. 'The enemy will be asleep. And we'll have the advantage of surprise.'

Hana and I nodded.

'One more thing,' Yorio said, resting his fingers lightly on my wrist. 'If we're separated, try to make your way back here to the *dojo*. Master Jin's plan is that we should gather here and wait until morning for news.'

'And if no one comes back?' I said, a sudden dread gripping my soul.

Yorio looked solemn. 'In that case, the few survivors must escape across the border when they can—to carry on the fight at the next time and place when Lord Hidehira attacks.'

Shortly after, we all began to move out. Students and villagers stood shoulder-to-shoulder, brothers in arms as they filed silently out of the courtyard. They formed a long line which began to wind slowly down the narrow pathways that led through the woods. The light of the dying day picked up the dull gleam of a helmet here, or a curve of *kote* sleeve armour.

I had an impression of an overwhelming number of men and boys, their faces darkened with mud, moving in a solid mass towards their common goal—Hidehira, the enemy. And though we were marching into battle, I felt safe for the first time in many moons. I was surrounded by an army. An army of friends. I had Hana one side of me, Yorio on the other side, and Yorio's friends at my back. We were led by Master Jin, a trusted friend of Master Goku's.

Could it be that our troubles were almost at an end?

Perhaps tonight we would be victorious. Perhaps tonight would be the night when I exacted my revenge. We would defeat Uncle Hidehira and his troops, rescue Mother and Moriyasu, and restore honour to the name of Yamamoto. And then, I promised myself silently, I would track down Tatsuya's captors and rescue my friend.

We slipped through the wood and gathered at the curve of the river, silent as ghosts. More farmers and peasants joined us, all dressed in dark clothes, their faces smeared with mud. I was surprised at how many people there were— hundreds willing to risk their lives to stand against Uncle.

We moved on, cutting across the valley towards the town. The watchtowers loomed up in the darkness ahead, and beyond them stood the *shinden* with its prickly-looking roof. I caught glimpses of movement along the tops of the watchtowers, and the occasional flicker of light.

'Sentries,' whispered Yorio. 'Our *jito* has posted them throughout the town, but especially along the barriers. They'll be preparing for a siege.' He grinned, his teeth flashing white in the darkness. 'They don't know we're here to help them. We'll attack, and pray to the Buddha that they aim their arrows at Hidehira's men and not at us!'

Treading cautiously, we moved on towards the enemy encampment. The first thing I saw was the glow of a camp-fire, then a dozen or more horses tied to posts, and beyond them hundreds of white tents huddled together beneath the town walls.

Uncle Hidehira's men will be in those tents, I thought with satisfaction, *sleeping in preparation for their dawn attack.*

But then my heart thumped, because as we drew closer I could see that far from being a sleeping village of quiet tents, the army encampment was a hive of activity. Lanterns had been lit and strung from iron stands. Samurai were everywhere—fastening armour, sharpening swords, fitting iron helmets onto their heads.

Hana reached out and grasped my wrist. 'The attack is not tomorrow,' she said in an urgent whisper. 'The scouts made a mistake. Those soldiers are preparing to go into battle now!'

Yorio's jaw hardened. 'You're right,' he murmured.

Around me, villagers and students were silently drawing their weapons. Keeping low, we slipped into camp, ducking under tent ropes and skirting lantern stands. Somewhere a horse whinnied. I saw one of Yorio's friends—Norio—rise up behind a samurai who was strapping on a piece of sleeve armour. A blade flashed and there was a spurt of blood, black in the darkness.

The samurai sagged at the knees. Norio lowered him to the ground.

The kill had taken less time than three of my heartbeats.

Other students rose up out of the darkness, silently, like ninja. They dispatched four or five samurai, blades glittering in the lantern-light. The smell of blood and sweat caught in my nostrils.

Then one of Uncle Hidehira's battle-hardened warriors spotted us . . .

Bellowing loudly, he snatched up a spear and advanced.

The lone warrior was met by a wave of students. Steel clashed on steel. I could hear a warning cry rippling out across the darkness. Other soldiers came running, snatching up weapons, some of them still fastening their breastplates. Master Jin's army poured in from all sides to join the slaughter, no need for stealth now.

In the confusion, Hana grabbed my hand and

we slipped away. 'Now's our chance. We must find Mother and Moriyasu.'

We crept between the tents, ducking at intervals to cast glances inside. Hidehira's soldiers ignored us. They were running back and forth, shouting frenzied battle cries as they wielded their swords. Suddenly a hail of arrows came out of the sky, like rain, and I knew that the sentries on the town wall were coming in on the side of the students.

In the midst of the chaos I spotted a large tent with lavish red and gold banners hanging either side of the entrance. It had to be Uncle's!

'Over there,' I said to Hana. But before we could make a move in that direction, the flaps of the tent were pushed open and a figure in full samurai armour came running out, sword in hand.

'Manabu,' Hana whispered hastily, pulling me back into the shadow of a nearby tent. His eyes glistened, and I could see that he was eager to spill blood.

As the tent flaps rippled closed behind Manabu, I caught a glimpse of Mother and Moriyasu. They were on their knees in the middle of the tent, hands tied behind their backs, shoulders bowed in defeat.

'They're alive!' I felt as if I could fly. 'We have to rescue them,' I said to Hana, as soon as Manabu was gone. 'Come on!'

We left the shadows and raced across the clearing. I ducked into the tent and found myself face-to-face with a fierce-looking samurai guard!

He was more surprised than I was, and it gave me the advantage. Swinging my sword high, I sliced through the strap of his horned helmet and cut his throat. His eyes bulged and he made a wheezing sound. But I was already past him. I caught a glimpse of Hana clashing with a second guard. She dispatched him without a word, her face pale and terrible.

Together we ran to Mother and Moriyasu. They both stared at us in disbelief as we dropped to our knees and began to untie them. Fingers fumbling, I tore the ropes from Mother's wrists and fell into her arms.

'I'm sorry,' I wept. 'So sorry. I'm sorry I couldn't choose you!'

As Hana freed little Moriyasu, my mother held me close. 'Hush,' she said softly, stroking my hair. 'Hush, Kimi. Do not weep. I understand what you did, and why.'

Moriyasu flung himself at us, stretching his arms around Hana and Mother and me, burying his face in our kimonos. 'We are all together again,' he said, his voice small and muffled.

After a few moments, Mother pulled away. 'We can't stay here,' she said. 'Hidehira's arrival is imminent. We must get away before he comes. He will be bringing an army with him.'

'Isn't there an army here already?' I asked in astonishment.

'When Hidehira gets here, the army will triple in size,' Mother said. Rising, she hurried across to the far side of the tent and selected two swords from a stand of weapons. Then she turned to look at Hana and me. 'We will all protect Moriyasu,' she said firmly. 'Whatever else happens, we must get him out of here alive.'

Hana and I nodded. We kept our little brother between us as we made our way out of the tent.

Outside, we found ourselves in the midst of a frenzied battlefield. The clang of steel blades echoed in the night air, broken by hoarse cries and the hammer of iron on wood. Several wounded samurai lurched past us. One of them was missing an ear, another had a gaping hole where his eye should have been.

Suddenly, a soldier wearing one of Uncle's red silk *mon* badges came rushing at us from the left. He swung his sword in a slanting curve. I would have met him with a block—but before I could move, Mother was there! Her long hair swung like silk as she blocked him, twisted, and attacked.

Steel flashed by the light of a nearby lantern, and the samurai fell onto one knee. He groaned and clutched at his stomach.

I stared at my mother with renewed respect. I had often seen her practising with Father, but I had not realized how skilful she was or how lethal she could be. I had never seen her hurt anyone. Shaking myself, I moved quickly, plunging forward. We fought our way through the battleground, trying to keep a protective ring around Moriyasu.

Mother moved as well with the blade as Hana and I, cutting Uncle's soldiers down with a quiet strength. Soon our swords were bloodied and red. Around us, the fighting intensified as more and more villagers and students poured in from the surrounding area, howling as they rushed to the kill.

We ducked and weaved, stepping over the dead as we headed for the edge of the encampment.

'Where are we going, Kimi?' Mother asked breathlessly, her stained blade held in a two-handed grip.

'We must make for the river,' I told her. 'From

there we can find our way back up to the *dojo*. Master Jin told everyone to gather there and wait for news.'

Mother gave a sharp nod and twisted around to fend off an attack from a bare-headed samurai with wild eyes. Their swords clashed. Mother shifted her centre of gravity and powered upwards, kicking the man hard in the chest. He staggered backwards, caught his foot on a tent rope, and lost his balance.

The samurai had hardly touched the floor before we were fleeing.

'This way!' cried Hana, leading little Moriyasu by the hand as she hurried between two tents. Beyond, I could see open countryside and a pathway that I knew would lead eventually to the river.

We were almost there. Almost free!

A dark figure stepped out from the shadows, blocking our way. He had a blade in each hand and murder in his eyes. My heart squeezed tight with fear, and I let out a shocked gasp.

It was Manabu.

Chapter 20

Manabu launched himself at us, blade slashing down in a silver arc.

Hana thrust Moriyasu behind her as I leapt forward to meet Manabu's strike, my sword singing.

Manabu let out a blood-curdling cry that carried across the camp. At once, several samurai came rushing to his aid. One battle-scarred warrior hacked at Mother, but she met him with a high block. Another slashed at Hana, who quickly deflected his blade and thrust a cut in towards his throat.

I turned my attention to Manabu, engaging him in a deadly battle. His yellow teeth glistened as they caught the glow of a nearby lantern. 'I should have killed you myself while I had the chance,' he sneered, bringing his sword down in a deadly curve.

'Well, you didn't,' I said, blocking him with an upward swing. 'And now I've come to kill you, instead.'

Manabu's face darkened with rage. He cut left and right. I avoided each of his strikes, then bent at the knees and executed a fast two-handed slice. He leapt back, and then feinted—first one way, then the other.

For a moment, I tried to read him. Then a memory flashed into my mind of my fight with Yorio on the riverbank. My father's words whispered through my mind. *Hush your thoughts, Kimi . . .*

The only way I could be victorious was if I could find the peace inside myself.

Manabu and I danced around each other. My gaze was fixed on the whole of his body, his centre. He feinted again, but this time I was ready. I would not be fooled into acting. I stood firm, my blade held high.

Manabu feinted again. Again, I held back. His gaze darted to Hana, who was cutting and parrying, battling hard with a seasoned warrior who grunted as he attacked. Moriyasu was behind her, his face pale.

Suddenly Manabu dropped the sword he was holding in his left hand. His arm flashed out, and he caught Moriyasu by his kimono. Moriyasu yelped and struggled. But there was nothing he could do. Manabu held him tightly.

Holding my brother at arm's length like a half-drowned kitten, Manabu cast me a triumphant stare. 'Drop your weapon,' he snarled, 'or I kill the boy.'

My heart was racing, my breathing ragged. But I steadied myself.

Find the strength within you, Kimi . . .

With my father's words still echoing through my soul, I leaped forward. With a twirling slice, I brought my blade down hard. The steel sang, alive in my hand, as it went through hardened leather armour, into flesh and bone—the arm that clung to my little brother.

As his severed arm fell to the ground, Manabu let out a yell that shredded the night air around us. He clutched at his shoulder. Blood pumped out from the gaping wound and he fell to his knees, grey-faced and moaning.

Justice had been done. He had deceived us for

so long and now he would live the rest of his life one-armed.

But Moriyasu was free. He rushed to me and buried his face in my side with a whimper. I put my arm around him and held him tight. 'It's all right, little brother,' I said gently. 'You're safe now.'

Beside me, Mother dispatched her opponent with a sudden slash. The enemy fell to the ground, groaning. Shaking the blood from her blade, my mother turned to me, her face grim. But before she could speak, a conch horn blared on the far side of the camp. The thunder of horses' hooves made the ground shake.

An army of battle-ready samurai came pouring between the tents like a swarm of locusts, their red and gold silk banners flying.

'Uncle is coming,' Hana said in horror.

I caught a glimpse of Yorio, racing towards us. Behind him, an enormous ebony horse reared. Uncle was sitting astride it, his face a mask of venom. His armour gleamed and his crimson robes rippled as he slashed his sword left and right, dispatching students and villagers with ease.

I pushed Moriyasu behind me. 'We must help our friends,' I said breathlessly.

But in the next moment, Yorio reached us. He

turned me round, propelling me towards the dark edges of the encampment. 'Go,' he urged us. 'Get out of here now, all of you.'

I caught a glimpse of Uncle in his terrifying horned helmet, directing his horse over the body of a slain villager. The muscular beast pranced and reared, trampling the dead underfoot.

I shook Yorio's hand from my arm. 'Your people need help,' I insisted. 'We must fight with you.'

'No,' Yorio said, shaking his head. 'Moriyasu must get to safety—he must be ready to take Hidehira's place.'

'Your friend is right, Kimi,' Mother said, ramming her bloodied blade into its sheath. 'Come, we must leave this place before Hidehira sees us.'

Hana nodded. 'If he gives chase on that horse, then we cannot hope to out-run him,' she said.

I held Yorio's gaze for a moment. He nodded. 'I will do it. Go, Kimi,' he said. 'We will meet again, you and I.'

Yorio turned and raced back into battle, towards Uncle on his horse, sword swinging. I caught my breath as he cut down first one opponent and then another. Watching him, I wondered how we could ever repay all these people who had helped us on our journey. The *ronin* captain; the fisherman and his family; Master Jin; Yorio; and of course our dear friend Tatsuya, who was out there *somewhere*. We would have to find him somehow, and rescue him from the ninja.

Hana's fingers touched my own, dragging me back to reality. 'Come on, Kimi,' she said. 'We must get Moriyasu to a safe place.'

Uncle Hidehira's soldiers began to pour towards the walled town, bellowing their battle cries. Swords clashed and arrows sang as they cut the air.

My heart ached as I turned away. But I knew that it was right for us to leave now. Hana and I had achieved what we had come for. We had rescued Mother and Moriyasu. We were a family again.

We set our backs to the carnage and headed for the river . . . and freedom.

Epilogue

That night, we left the battlefield knowing that the town would fall.

Hidehira's army would overcome the *shinden*. Samurai would stream through the streets. The people would be slaughtered. And the *jito*, the Lord Steward of this part of Sagami, would be murdered.

Hidehira would seize the estates. Piece by piece, Uncle would take over the lands.

Meanwhile, we would be fugitives. Together as a family once more, but still on the run.

That day, as Hana and I reached the riverbank with

Mother and Moriyasu, a soft spring rain began to fall. I tilted my face up towards the sky, letting the warm droplets splash away the blood that streaked my skin and clotted my hair.

But when the stain of combat had been washed away, my tears remained. I knew in my heart that only the blood of my uncle could wash away my family's grief.

Turn the page for a preview of the next thrilling
part of Kimi and Hana's story…

Between Heaven and Earth

Available in
September 2012

Soldiers! They're here!'
Yoshiki burst into the room, roughly sliding open the screen so that it made us jump. For these few days, he had been careful not to draw attention to us. Things had to be bad for him to be so reckless now.

He dropped to his knees in the centre of the room and started to pull up floorboards. His face was red and shiny with sweat. Understanding the danger, I threw myself to the ground and grappled with a board, heaving until it gave way.

'Are you sure?' I asked.

'They're looking for something, for . . . you, I think,' he said. 'There's no other reason they could have come back.' Our eyes locked. We both knew that this was life or death. And not only for my family and me. Yoshiki and the whole village could be killed if we were discovered.

'Thank you,' I said.

Yoshiki nodded and glanced at Moriyasu. Our brother had been woken by the disturbance. Mother stirred behind him. I realized that Yoshiki shared our hopes—that one day Moriyasu, our father's rightful heir, would grow up to return these estates to stability and happiness.

'Don't thank me,' Yoshiki said, turning back. 'Just try to stay alive.'

Mother and Moriyasu scrambled to their feet. Mother's hands trembled as she pulled her robe tight around her waist and accepted the sword that Yoshiki held out to her. Little Moriyasu bit his lip, trying not to show his fear.

'I usually store rice down here, but there's none left,' Yoshiki explained. 'It will make a good hiding place for you.'

Outside, we could hear screams and cries for help among terse voices issuing commands. Looking out through the main room, I saw a woman dragged past the open screen by a samurai soldier. The thick leather panels of his armour glistened in the sunlight and the bronze trim on his iron helmet shone dangerously. If he had turned his head, he would have seen us.

There was no time to waste.

I scrambled into the shallow dirt cavity and reached for my sister, pulling her down beside me. Moriyasu leaped in next to us. Mother gracefully stepped down, Yoshiki holding her hand to steady her.

'Stay calm, my children,' she said, lying on the packed earth beside us.

Then the wooden floorboards were put back in place over our heads.

It felt as though we were being buried alive.

My arms were pinned to my sides by the bodies of my sister and brother and the air was thick with the scent of wood, so close to our faces. Yoshiki threw a mat over where we were hiding and dust settled onto us. My eyes itched with grit, forcing slow tears to streak down either side of my face. I couldn't move to wipe them away. I licked my lips nervously and immediately regretted it as dirt filled my mouth. *Stay strong*, I willed myself. Moriyasu let out a quiet sob.

'Sit there, my sweet one,' I heard Yoshiki say gently above. 'Try not to move.'

'Why?' a small voice asked. It was Sakura, Yoshiki's daughter. The innkeeper was using his own daughter as a decoy. We heard the floor-boards shift as Sakura came to take her place on the mat above our heads. I promised myself that one day I would repay this innocent girl, caught in the chase.

Heavy footsteps sounded nearby—confident, aggressive, and determined. Fate had arrived at our doorway. I twisted my wrist so that my finger-tips could brush against the back of Hana's hand.

'Are you the innkeeper?' a deep voice demand-ed. I heard Yoshiki fall to his knees in front of the man. I could just see Yoshiki's flushed face through a crack between the floorboards.

'I am,' he acknowledged.

'Ten bags of rice from each village are to be bestowed upon the esteemed Lord Steward Yamamoto. Hand over your rice immediately.'

'I am sorry, sir, but I have nothing for you. All our rice has long gone to the Lord Steward. We are destitute.' I admired Yoshiki for the calm-ness of his speech. The soldier would almost cer-tainly have his hand on his sword.

'I don't believe you!' shouted the soldier, enraged.

A sudden scuffling sound made me catch my breath.

'Father!' Sakura cried out above us.

Yoshiki's feet dragged on the floorboards as he was pulled across the room.

'Show me your supplies!' I could imagine the spittle landing on Yoshiki's cheeks. Yoshiki was thrown out of the little room, footsteps following him.

Silence fell, though I could hear my heart pumping hard in my chest. I waited for a movement from Sakura; for her to run after her father. She shifted her weight uneasily above us, but stayed put.

'Father?' she whispered into the empty room. I wished I could comfort her. But there was no comfort to be had for any of us.

I could hear my brother whispering a prayer. A bead of sweat ran down my temple and into my ear. But there was no more sign of the soldiers. Perhaps we had been lucky. I dared to breathe a sigh of relief.

Then the door screens were ripped down and Moriyasu jumped beside me. Men ran into the room and I heard Sakura cry out as the table in the corner was turned over and clay pots slammed against the walls. I could imagine how easily the modest furniture was being smashed to pieces.

'Pull this place apart!' a deep voice ordered. 'These people will not hide anything from us. Get the girl out of the way!'

Feet paced across the floor.

'Please, no! I beg you; do not harm my daughter,' Yoshiki's words rang out. There was a dull thud and a small cry as thick leather smacked against small ribs—then a crash. I knew that Sakura had been kicked into something above us.

I bit my lip hard. The iron tang of blood filled my mouth. I heard Yoshiki being dragged across the room and then could see him being hurled to the floor.

'Stay out of our way,' someone said, before spitting on the floor beside the innkeeper. Yoshiki's humiliation was complete and it was all our fault. He turned his face and his eyes met mine through the sliver of space that had become my window on the world. His gaze remained steady for a moment, then he turned his face to the floor.

'Look!' someone cried out. 'The fool's given away his hiding place. He was looking over there!' Heavy feet stomped over, then the mat was tossed aside and the rickety floorboards above our faces shuddered.

'No, you misunderstand,' Yoshiki tried to protest. 'There is nothing here; I promise you.' Someone paced across the room and slapped a hand across Yoshiki's face, making him cry out. Dirt rained down on us as a soldier grappled with the corner of a floorboard and I heard his gasp of satisfaction as the board came up and he threw it to one side.

He thrust his face into the space beside us. The man squinted and blinked. We had become accustomed to the musty dark, but after the bright midday sun, this samurai could see nothing. Blindly he thrust a hand into the cavity. His calloused hands felt the air in front of my face, and I pressed my lips together. I could not let him feel even the whisper of my breath on his fingertips.

Impatiently he reared back and tore at a second floorboard. I could hear Mother whispering a reassurance to Moriyasu. Beside me, Hana continued to stare straight up, her eyes unwavering.

The second floorboard broke in two as it gave way. The soldier's head and shoulders lunged down . . .